GRAMMAR OF LOVE

CLASSICS OF RUSSIAN LITERATURE

GRAMMAR OF LOVE

BY IVAN BUNIN

Translated

By John Cournos

HYPERION PRESS, INC.
Westport, Connecticut

/55375

Published in 1934 by Harrison Smith and Robert Haas, New Yo
Copyright 1934 by Harrison Smith and Robert Haas, Inc.
Hyperion reprint edition 1977
Library of Congress Catalog Number 76-23876
ISBN 0-88355-481-X (cloth ed.)
ISBN 0-88355-482-8 (paper ed.)
Printed in the United States of America

Library of Congress Cataloging in Publication Data

Bunin, Ivan Alekseevich, 1870 -
    Grammar of love.

    *(Classics of Russian literature) (The Hyperion
library of world literature)*
    *Reprint of the ed. published by H. Smith and R. Haas,
New York.*
    CONTENTS: Sunstroke. — Ida. — Meteor. [etc.]
    I. Title.
PZ3.B8835Gr17 [PG3453.B9]   891.7'3'3   76-23876
ISBN 0-88355-481-X
ISBN 0-88355-482-8 pbk.

CONTENTS

Grateful acknowledgment is extended to the following magazines in which two of the stories in this volume first appeared: to *Story* for "A Simple Peasant"; to *The Yale Review* for "On the Great Road."

SUNSTROKE

THEY had had their dinner, and they left the brilliantly lighted dining-room and went on deck, where they paused by the rail. She closed her eyes and, palm turned outward, pressing her hand to her cheek, laughed with unaffected charm. Everything was charming about this little woman. She said:

"I'm quite intoxicated. . . . Or I've gone wholly out of my mind. Where did you drop down from? But three hours ago I scarcely suspected your existence. I don't even know where you came on board. Was it in

Samara? Well, it doesn't matter, my dear. Really, my head's in a whirl, or is it the boat turning?"

Before them was darkness—and lights. Out of the darkness a strong soft breeze blew in their faces, while the lights glided past them: with Volga friskiness the steamer cut a sharp curve, as it approached the small pier.

The lieutenant took her hand, lifting it to his lips. The strong small hand smelt of sunburn. Bliss and anguish caused his heart to grow tremulous at the thought that underneath this light linen dress she was doubtless all strong and tanned after a whole month's lying under the southern sun upon the hot sea sands (she had said she was coming from Anapu). The lieutenant murmured: "Let's get off here. . . ."

"Where?" she asked in astonishment.

"Here, on this pier."

"Why?"

He was silent. Again she laid the back of her hand upon her hot cheek.

"You're mad. . . ."

"Let's get off," he repeated dully. "I implore you. . . ."

"*Akh*, do as you like," she said, turning away.

The moving steamer crashed with a dull thud against the dimly lighted pier, and the pair almost fell upon each other. The end of a cable came flying above their

4

heads, then the ship receded and the water clamorously seethed, the gang-plank rattled. . . . The lieutenant ran for the luggage.

Presently they passed through the tiny drowsy pier shed and, once out of doors, found themselves ankle-deep in sand; in silence they seated themselves in the dust-covered hackney cab. The ascent of the steep road, soft with dust, punctuated with infrequent lamp-posts standing awry, seemed endless. At last they emerged on top, the carriage rattled along a paved street; here was a square, some administrative buildings, a belfry, the warmth and the smells of a summer night in a provincial town. . . . The cabby stopped before a lighted entrance; through the open doors could be seen the steep wooden stairway. An old unshaven servant in a pink shirt and frock-coat reluctantly took their bags and went forward on his tired feet. They entered a large but terribly stuffy room still hot from the day's sun, its windows hung with white curtains, its mirror-topped mantelpiece decorated with two unused candles —and no sooner had they entered and the servant closed the door upon them than the lieutenant impetuously flung himself upon her and they both lost themselves in a kiss of such agonizing rapture that the moment was long to be remembered by them: nothing like it had ever been experienced by either one or the other.

At ten o'clock the next morning, a morning hot and

sunny and gay with the ringing of church bells, with the humming in the market-place facing the hotel, with the smell of hay and tar and all those complex odors with which every provincial Russian town reeks, she, this nameless little woman, for she refused to reveal her name, jestingly calling herself the lovely stranger, left him, resuming her journey. They had slept little, but when she emerged from behind the screen near the bed, within five minutes all washed and dressed, she looked as fresh as a seventeen-year-old girl. Was she embarrassed? Very little. As before, she was simple, gay and—quite rational.

"No, no, my dear," she said in response to his suggestion that they pursue the journey together. "No, you must remain here until the next boat. If we go on together, everything will be spoiled. I wouldn't like that. Please believe me, I'm not at all the sort of woman I may have led you to think. All that happened here never happened before and never will again. It's as if I suffered an eclipse. . . . Or, to be more precise, it's as if we both experienced something in the nature of a sunstroke. . . ."

The lieutenant rather lightly agreed with her. In gay happy spirits he escorted her in a carriage to the pier, which they reached just as the rose-tinted steamer was on the point of departure, and, on deck, in the presence of other passengers, he kissed her, and barely managed to jump on to the already receding gang-plank.

With the same lightness of spirit he returned to the hotel. Yet something had changed. Their room without her seemed quite different. It was still full of her—and empty. That was strange! It still smelt of her excellent English eau-de-cologne, her unfinished cup was still on the tray, but she was no longer there. . . . And the lieutenant's heart suddenly felt such tremors of tenderness that he made haste to smoke and, slapping his boot-leg with a crop, he paced up and down the room.

"A strange occurrence!" he said aloud, laughing, yet conscious of tears in his eyes. " 'Please believe me, I'm not at all the sort of woman I may have led you to think. . . .' And now she's gone. . . . An absurd woman!"

The screen was pushed to one side, the bed had not yet been made. And he felt that now he simply hadn't the courage to look upon this bed. He arranged the screen around it, closed the window that he might avoid hearing the market hum and the creaking of cart wheels, lowered the blown-out white curtains, and sat down on the divan. . . . Well, so that was the end to the "chance encounter"! She was gone—and was now far away, doubtless sitting in the glassed-in white salon or on deck, gazing at the immense sun-glinting river, at the passing barges, the yellow sand-banks, the distant radiance of water and sky, at the whole immeasurable expanse of the Volga. . . . And farewell, for ever, for eternity. . . . For how could they ever meet again? "I can't, after all," he mused, "for one reason or another, visit the town where her husband is, and her three-year-old daughter, and the rest of her family, the place where she leads her everyday life!"—And that town suddenly appeared to him as a most exceptional, a forbidden town, and the thought that she would go on living in it her lonely life, perhaps frequently remembering him, remembering their chance transient encounter, while he would never see her again, this thought stunned and unmanned him. No, this could not be! It was wholly absurd, unnatural, incredible! And he felt such anguish, such futility of existence in the years to come, that he was seized with terror, with despair.

"What the devil!" he thought, rising, and, again pacing up and down the room, he tried to avoid the sight of the bed behind the screen. "What's the matter with me? Who'd have thought it possible that the first time—and there. . . . What is there about her, and what exactly has happened? Really, it is as if it were some sort of sunstroke! But the main thing is, how am I to spend the whole day without her in this God-forsaken place?"

He vividly remembered her as she was, with all her most intimate traits; he remembered the smell of her sunburn and of her linen dress, of her strong body, the live, simple, gay sound of her voice. . . . The mood of but lately experienced delights of her feminine loveliness, was still singularly strong upon him; nevertheless, the main thing was another altogether new mood —that strange, incomprehensible mood, non-existent while they were still together, a mood which he could not have even imagined yesterday, when he first made this new, merely diverting, as he had thought, acquaintance, and concerning which he could no longer speak to anyone, no, not to anyone! "Yes, the main thing," he went on thinking, "is that you'll never be able to talk about it! And what is one to do, how is one to pass this endless day, with these memories, with this intolerable anguish, in this God-forsaken little town by that same radiant Volga, upon whose waters this rose-tinted steamer has borne her away!"

It was necessary to save himself, to occupy himself with something, to find amusement, to go somewhere. He resolutely put his cap on; strode vigorously, clinking his spurs, down the empty corridors; ran down the steep stairway toward the entrance. . . . Well, where should he go? At the entrance was a young cabby in a smart peasant's coat, calmly smoking a tiny cigar, apparently waiting for someone. The lieutenant glanced at him in distraught wonder: how was it possible for anyone to sit so calmly on a coach-box, and smoke, and seem so unconcerned, so indifferent? "Evidently, in this whole town I alone am so terribly unhappy," he thought, turning in the direction of the market-place.

The market was dispersing. Unwittingly he trod upon the fresh manure among the wagons, among the cart-loads of cucumbers, among the new pots and pans, and the women, who sat on the ground, vied with one another in trying to call his attention to their pots, which they took in their hands and made ring with their fingers, demonstrating their quality, while the peasants dinned in his ears: "Here are first-class cucumbers, Your Honor!" All this was stupid, absurd, and he ran from the place. He entered the church, where chanting was going on; it was loud and cheerful and determined, as if the chanters were conscious of the fulfilment of a duty; then he strode on through the streets, and in the heat of the sun wandered along the paths of a tiny neglected garden on the slope of a hill, overlooking the broad river with its splendor as of glinting steel. The shoulder-straps and buttons of his white summer uniform grew so hot that it was impossible to touch them. The inner band of his cap was wet with perspiration, his face flamed. . . .

On returning to the hotel he found delicious relief in the shelter of the large, empty, cool dining-room;

he removed his cap, sat down at a little table before an open window, through which the heat blew—a breeze for all that—and ordered an iced soup of pot-herbs. Everything was good, in everything there was immeasurable happiness, intense joy, even in this sultriness and in these market smells; in the whole unfamiliar little town and in this old provincial hotel it was present, this happiness, and, with it all, his heart was simply being rent into shreds. He drank several small glasses of vodka, and made a snack of pickled cucumbers, and he felt that without the least faltering he would choose to die tomorrow, if only by some miracle he could return her and spend but this one day with her—if only to have a chance to tell her and somehow prove to her, persuade her of his harrowing and marvelous love. . . . But why prove it to her? Why persuade her? He could not tell why, yet it seemed more necessary than life itself.

"My nerves are playing me pranks!" he thought, as he poured himself a fifth glass of vodka.

He consumed an entire small decanter, hoping in intoxication to forget, to bring to an end his agonized exultation. But no, it only grew more intense.

He pushed away the cold herb soup, asked for black coffee, and began to smoke and resolutely to deliberate upon ways and means of freeing himself from this unexpected, sudden love. But to free himself—he felt this acutely—was impossible. And, suddenly, with a rapid movement, he rose, picked up his cap and crop, and, asking where the post-office was, quickly went in the direction indicated, with the phrasing of a telegram already in his head: "Henceforth my life is wholly yours, unto death, to do with what you will." On reaching the thick-walled house, which sheltered the post and telegraph office, he paused in horror: he knew the town where she lived, he knew that she had a husband and a three-year-old daughter, but he knew neither her first name nor her surname! Several times in the course of the evening he had asked her, and each time she laughed and said:

"Why must you know who I am? I am Maria Green, Fairyland Queen. . . . Or simply the lovely stranger. . . . Isn't that enough for you?"

On the corner, near the post-office, was a photographic show-case. He looked steadily at a large portrait of a military man with elaborate epaulettes, with bulging eyes and low forehead, with surprisingly magnificent whiskers and expansive chest, all decorated with orders. . . . How absurdly ridiculous, how horribly ordinary it all was, because his heart had been vanquished—yes, vanquished, he understood it now—by this terrible "sunstroke," this intense love, this intense happiness! He glanced at a bridal couple—a young man in a long frock-coat and white neck-tie, his

hair cut in hedge-hog style; on his arm, in bridal veil,—
but he then diverted his gaze to the portrait of a good-
looking, spirited girl in a student's cap perched awry.
. . . Then, tormented by a harrowing envy toward all
these strangers, *non-suffering* human beings, he began
to look fixedly down the street.

"Where can I go? What can I do?" the insoluble,
oppressive question persisted in his mind and soul.

The street was deserted. The houses were all alike,
white, two-storied, middle-class, with large gardens,
and they gave the appearance of being uninhabited; a
thick white dust covered the pavement; all this dazzled; everything was drenched with the hot, flaming,
joyous, seemingly aimless sunshine. In the distance the
street rose, humped and pressed against the pure,
cloudless, grayish horizon, reflecting lilac. There was
something southern in this, reminiscent of Sebastopol,
Kertch . . . Anapu. The thought of the last was particularly unbearable. And the lieutenant, with lowered
head, screwing up his eyes against the light, with fixed
gaze on the ground, reeling, stumbling, spur catching
on spur, retraced his footsteps.

He returned to the hotel, shattered with fatigue, as
if he had performed a long journey in Turkestan or
the Sahara. Gathering his last strength, he entered his
large, desolate room. The room had already been
cleaned, and her last traces removed—only a solitary

hair-pin, forgotten by her, lay on the tiny table by the bed! He took off his jacket and glanced in the mirror: his face—the ordinary face of an officer, swarthy from sunburn, with whitish sun-bleached moustaches and bluish-white eyes, seeming against the sunburn whiter than they were—now showed a distraught, insane expression, and in his thin white shirt with standing starched collar there was something youthful and infinitely pathetic. He lay down on the bed, on his back, and rested his dust-covered boots on the footboard. The windows were open, the curtains lowered, and from time to time the light breeze filled them, blowing into the room sultriness and the odor of hot roofs and of all that luminous, now quite desolate, mute, unpeopled world of the Volga. He lay with his arms under his head and gazed fixedly into space. His head held the dim picture of the remote south, of the sun, the sea, Anapu, and it was something fabulous—as if the town to which she had gone, the town in which she had doubtless already arrived, was like no other town— and with it all there ripened the persistent thought of suicide. He closed his eyes, and felt on his cheeks the trickle of pungent, hot tears—and at last fell asleep. When he again opened his eyes there was already visible, through the curtains, the darkening reddish evening sun. The breeze had died down, the room was stuffy and dry, as in a wind-furnace. . . . And he remembered yesterday and this morning precisely as if they had been ten years ago.

In no great haste he rose, in no great haste washed himself; then he pulled the curtains aside, rang for the servant, asked for a samovar and his bill, and for a long time he drank tea with lemon. Then he ordered a cab and had his luggage taken out, and, seating himself in the reddish, burnt-out seat of the carriage, he gave the servant a whole five rubles as a tip.

"It looks, Your Honor, as though I brought you here last night!" said the cabby cheerfully, as he seized the reins.

When they reached the pier, the blue summer night already darkened above the Volga and many varicolored flames were scattered upon the river and flames hung in the mast of the approaching steamer.

"Got you here just in time!" said the cabby ingratiatingly.

The lieutenant also gave him five rubles, then with ticket in hand went to the pier. . . . Even as yesterday there was the soft sound of the hawsers, and the light dizziness from the vacillation under foot; then came the flying end of the cable, the clamor of the seething waters under the wheels of the steamer receding from the impact. . . . And the sight of the much-peopled steamer, ablaze with light, and the smells of its kitchens, seemed to extend a warm welcome.

Another minute, and the steamer was under way, going up the river, in the direction in which it had borne her away that same morning.

Ahead of it, the dark summer sunset was rapidly fading; gloomily, dreamily and iridescently, it was reflected in the river, showing patches glimmering with tremulous ripples in the distance under the sunset, and the flames scattered in the darkness round the steamer went on receding and receding.

The lieutenant sat under cover on deck, conscious of having aged by ten years.

IDA

ONCE during the Christmas holidays four of us breakfasted together—three old friends and a certain George Ivanovitch—at the Big Moscow Restaurant.

Owing to the holidays, the Big Moscow was empty and cool, fresh with the aroma of flowers, hyacinths and lily-of-the-valley. We walked through the old dining-hall and paused at the door of the new. We glanced around the tables newly decked with taut snow-white table covers in order to choose a spot which seemed to us the most comfortable. Radiant with cleanliness and courtesy, the steward made a modest and refined gesture toward the farthest corner, where stood a small round table with a semi-circular sofa, under a dense dark-green bay-tree. And we went there.

"Gentlemen," said the musical composer, making his way behind the table and flinging his squat torso on to the sofa—"gentlemen, I feel like giving you a treat in fine style.—Waiter," he said, addressing himself to the attendant, to whom he turned his broad peasant face with small narrow eyes, "spread for us your gayest cover. You know my kingly ways!"

"Why shouldn't I know? I had time to learn them by heart," replied, with a restrained smile, the shrewd waiter, who sported a small pure-silver beard. "You may depend upon me, I'll do my best. . . ." he added, as he placed an ash-tray before him.

And presently there appeared before them small glasses and goblets, bottles with variously colored liqueurs, pink salmon, swarthy-bodied sturgeon, a dish of opened shell-fish resting on splinters of ice, an orange cube of Cheshire cheese, a black glistening clod of pressed caviar, a white pail steaming with cold and filled with champagne. . . . Nevertheless, we began with vodka. The musical composer loved to do the pouring. He filled three glasses, then jestingly faltered:

"Most precious George Ivanovitch, may I also pour you one?"

George Ivanovitch, who had the sole and rather odd occupation—that of being the friend of well-known writers, artists and actors—was a very quiet, always well-disposed human being. He gently flushed, as was always his habit before saying anything, and answered with a certain heedlessness and ease of manner:

"By all means, most worthless Pavel Nikolaye-vitch!"

And the composer also filled his glass. Then he lightly clinked his glass with ours, and with a flourish and the words, "Best of luck!" took his liquor at one gulp and, with great gusto, went for the snacks. We too joined in, and spent a good while at this jolly business. Then we ordered some fish-soup and began to smoke. From the old dining-hall there suddenly came the gentle sad sounds of the reproachable musical machine. And the composer, leaning back in his seat, puffing away at a cigarette and, according to his habit, raising his chest and taking a deep breath, said:

"Friends, and all the more the pity because you are my esteemed friends, allow me to tell you that, notwithstanding the exceeding joy of my stomach, I feel very sad. And I feel sad because I've just suddenly remembered, on waking this morning, a little episode which occurred in the life of one of my friends—a positive ass, as it turned out afterwards—exactly three years ago, on the second day of the Christmas holidays. . . ."

"A little episode, and, no doubt at all, an amorous one," said George Ivanovitch with his girlish smile.

The composer glanced ask   e at him.

"Amorous?" he asked coo   and scornfully. "*Akh,* George Ivanovitch, George Ivanovitch, how will you answer for your depravity and merciless mind before the Last Judgment? Well, God have mercy on you! '*Je veux un trésor qui les contient tous, je veux la jeunesse!*' " raising his brows he joined with the tune of the machine, playing Faust, and, turning toward his companions, continued:

"My friends, this is the story. Once upon a time, in a certain kingdom, a certain maiden used to call at the house of a certain gentleman; she was a friend of his wife from university days, and she was so disingenuous, so charming, that the gentleman simply called her Ida, that is, by her first name. It was Ida and Ida, he did not even know her family name very well. He only knew that she came of a good but indigent family, that she was the daughter of a musician, a man once well-known as a conductor, that she lived with her parents and was waiting, as one may suppose, for a suitable man to turn up—and that was all. . . .

IDA

"How am I to describe Ida to you? The gentleman in question was warmly disposed to her, but of actual attention, I repeat, he showed her—well, to be exact, zero! She would come to the house—meeting her, he'd say: 'A-a, Ida, my dear! How are you, how are you? It's splendid to see you!' And she, in answer, would merely smile, take her hat off, touch her hair with both hands, hide her handkerchief in her muff; then, in a girlish way (and somewhat absurdly), she'd glance around: 'Is Masha at home?' 'At home, my dear, at home . . .' 'May I look in on her?' And calmly she would proceed through the dining-room in the direction of Masha's room. 'Masha,' she would call before the door, 'may I come in?'—The voice is deep, stirring one to the marrow. Add to this voice all the rest of it: the freshness of youth, of good health, the fragrance of the girl on entering the room from the frosty outdoor air . . . then her tallness, shapeliness, the rare harmony and naturalness of her movements. . . . Her face too was rare enough—at the first glance it seemed quite ordinary, but a closer look would cause you to admire: the tones of the skin were even, warm—they reminded you of the most perfect apple—and the color of her eyes was violet, alive. . . .

"Yes, give her a close look, and you're forced to admire. But this imbecile, that is the hero of our tale, would look at her and, flying into rapture, would say:

'*Akh*, Ida, Ida, you don't know your own price!'—he'd then see her answering, altogether charming, but as it were a not wholly attentive smile—and he'd leave her to go into his study, and he'd again be engaged in some sort of twaddle, so-called artistic creation, the devil take him!

"And thus time went on and on, and thus our gentleman did not once stop to give a serious thought to Ida and—can you conceive of it?—he actually failed to notice when one fine day Ida disappeared somewhere. There was simply no Ida, and he didn't even think to ask his wife: what in the heavens has become of our Ida? Now and then he did recall, and he felt as if something were lacking, and he imagined the sweet agony of putting an arm around her waist, and he mentally glimpsed her little gray muff, the color of her face and her violet eyes, her lovely arm, her English skirt. . . . He'd grow wistful for a little—then again he'd forget. Thus, a whole year passed, and another . . . When suddenly it became necessary for him to take a journey south. . . .

"It happened on Christmas day. For all that, the journey could not be delayed. And lo, bidding farewell to his thralls and domestics, our gentleman mounted a fleet steed and departed. He rode a day, he rode a night, and reached at last a railway junction, where it was necessary to change. He reached it, it is pertinent to observe, considerably delayed; hence, as soon the train began to slow down near the platform, he sprang from the train and, seizing the first porter he could get hold of by the collar, he shouted: 'Is that the express train going away there?' 'Yes, it's only just gone! After all, your train was a full hour and a half late,' replied the porter, with a polite smile. 'Is that true, you wretch? You aren't joking? What am I to do now? You deserve a sentence of hard labor, in Siberia! I'd send you to the block, I would!' 'Guilty, guilty,' replied the porter, 'even a sword wouldn't smite at this guilty head, Your Excellency. There's nothing to do but wait for the next train. . . .' And he humbly lowered his head and conducted our distinguished traveler to the station. . . .

"The station was full of people, and friendly, comfortable and warm. For a whole week there had been a snow-storm, everything on the railways was in a horrible mess, all instructions went to the devil, the junctions were overcrowded. The same condition, of course, prevailed here. Everywhere there were people and luggage, the buffets were open all day, and all day there were odors of food, and there were samovars and coffee; as everyone knows, not bad things during frosty days and snow-storms. Quite apart from that, this particular station was one of the better kind, and spacious, so that our traveler instantly felt that to re-

main here even a whole day wasn't such a misfortune.
'I'll put myself in shape, then treat myself to a
splendid repast and drink,' he thought with some pleasure as he entered the waiting-room and immediately
set to work to put his designs into execution. He shaved
and washed himself, donned a clean shirt and left the
dressing-room, feeling twenty years younger; he directed his steps toward the buffet. There he drank a
glass of vodka, and followed it with another. He consumed a patty, then a small fish, and was about to have
another drink, when suddenly behind him he heard
a strangely familiar feminine voice, the loveliest in the
world. At this point, of course, 'startled,' he turned
around—and whom do you suppose he saw before
him but Ida!

"Astonished and overjoyed, he could not at first
find words to say to her; he merely stared at her like
a sheep. As for her—well, she was a woman, you know
what that means—she did not as much as blink an eyelash. Naturally, she too could not help feeling astonished, and no doubt her face showed some of the
pleasure she felt; nevertheless, I must repeat, she preserved a superb calm. 'My dear,' she said, 'what fates
sent you here? What a pleasant meeting!' And her
eyes revealed that she spoke the truth, only now she
spoke with extraordinary simplicity, and not at all in

the manner in which she used to speak to him, well
. . . somewhat mockingly, shall I say?

"And our gentleman was put a bit out of counte-
nance too because also in other things Ida was altogether unrecognizable: marvelously she had bloomed
in every way, as some splendid flower blooms in the
purest water in some sort of crystal goblet, and her
attire corresponded to it: everything in good taste, and
coquettish too, a little winter hat which must have
cost a pretty penny, across her shoulders a thousand-
ruble sable cloak. . . . When our gentleman humbly
and awkwardly kissed her hand which dazzled with
precious stones, she lightly flung her head over her
shoulder and casually observed: 'Do, by the way,
meet my husband!'—and immediately, with a rapid
movement, there modestly stepped forth from behind
her a dashing young man, in the military manner, a
student. . . ."

"*Akh*, the insolent fellow!" interrupted George
Ivanovitch. "An ordinary student?"

"That's the point, my dear George Ivanovitch. He
wasn't ordinary," said the composer, with grim
derision. "It seems that never before or since has our
gentleman seen such a noble-looking youth, such a
fabulous face as if chiseled out of marble. And so
smartly dressed! A coat of the best light gray cloth,

such as only great dandies wear, fitting his harmonious torso like a glove; trousers with pantaloon-straps; a dark-green cap on the Prussian model; and an elegant great-coat with an otter collar. With it all, he was singularly appealing and modest. Ida murmured one of the most celebrated family names of Russia, while he quickly removed his cap with a hand attired in a chamois glove—the cap, of course, revealed a red moire lining, then quickly bared his other hand, a slender pale-blue hand, clicked his heels and deferentially bowed his small, meticulously brushed hair. 'So that's how it is!' thought our by now stupefied hero and once more glanced stupidly at Ida—and instantly, from the glance she let glide down the student's figure, it became clear that she, of course, was the queen, and he her slave, but by no means a simple slave, rather a slave who bore his thralldom with the greatest gratification and even with pride.—'Very, very pleased to make your acquaintance!' said this slave in the heartiest voice, pressing hard the outstretched hand, and, with a happy smile, straightened again. 'You must know, I'm an old admirer of yours, and have heard much about you from Ida,' he added, looking friendlily, and was about to launch into a further speech fitting to the occasion, when he was unexpectedly interrupted: 'Be quiet, Pete, don't embarrass me!' said Ida rapidly and turned to our gentleman: 'My dear, why, I haven't seen you in a thousand years! I'd like to talk to you for ever, but I haven't the least desire to talk in his presence. Our reminiscences wouldn't interest him, and it would only be a bore and that would be awkward. Let's you and me go along then and have our chat on the platform. . . .' And, having spoken, she took our divine slave under the arm and led him to the platform, up which she walked with him nearly a mile, until they got to a place where the snow reached almost to the knee, and—quite unexpectedly, she made a declaration there of her love for him. . . ."

"Really . . . her love for him. What do you mean?" we asked in a single voice, somewhat nonplussed.

Instead of making a reply, the composer once again drew in a deep breath, swelling out and raising his shoulders. He lowered his eyes and, awkwardly raising himself, extracted the bottle from the swishing-tinkling ice in the silver pail and poured himself a large goblet. His cheeks flushed, his short neck reddened. In the effort to hide his confusion, he drained the goblet at one go, as if it contained cider, and took up the tune of the machine in the next room: "*Laisse moi, laisse moi contempler ton visage!*"—but immediately broke off and, resolutely raising to us even more narrowed eyes, went on:

"Yes, just what I said . . . her love for him. . . .

And this declaration was, unhappily, of the most real and earnest kind. Was it stupid, mad, unexpected, incredible? Naturally, but all the same—a fact! It happened precisely as I am describing it to you. As they entered upon the platform she immediately in a hurried manner and simulated animation began to question him about Masha, how she was faring, and how her other common acquaintances in Moscow were faring, what gossip in general he had to give her, and so on. Then she informed him that she was already in the second year of her marriage, that she had lived with her husband partly in Petersburg, partly abroad, and partly on their country estate near Vitebsk. . . . Our gentleman merely hurried along with her and already entertained a premonition that there was something blowing ill in the wind, that he was on the eve of some imbecilic incredible event, and he stared at the whiteness of the snow-drifts, which had collected in an astonishing quantity and buried everything under them, —and he stared at the platforms, rail-beds, the roofs of the sheds, and at the red and green railway carriages stranded on all the ways. . . . He stared at it all and with a sinking heart comprehended but one thing: that, as it now appeared to him, he had for many years fiercely loved this same Ida.

"And then—can you imagine it?—something happened. It happened on one of the more remote side platforms, where Ida walked up toward some packing-cases, brushed off the snow from one of them with her muff and, raising toward our gentleman her paling face, her violet eyes, said to him breathlessly and with startling suddenness: 'And now, my dear, answer me still another question: Did you ever know and do you know now that I have loved you a whole five years and love you to this very day?' "

The musical machine, which up to now had been playing in the distance something vague and low, suddenly burst forth on a heroic scale, in solemn, stern tones. The composer lapsed into silence and directed upon us frightened, astonished eyes. Then he said in a low voice:

"Yes, that was what she said to him. . . . And now allow me to ask you: how is one to describe the scene in our absurd human words? What can I say to you except platitudes about this uplifted face, lighted up with the pallor of that singularly white snow, such as to be seen immediately after storms? What can I say to you of the inexplicably tender appearance of this face, so much like the freshness of the snow, or generally speaking of a face of a lovely young woman, who during a walk had breathed in so much of the snowy air and suddenly declared her love for you and was waiting for an answer from you to this declaration? What did I say of her eyes? Violet? No, no, that's no word for it, and where in the devil is one to get the right word? And those parted lips? And the expression, the combined expression, that is, of face, eyes and lips? And the long muff of sable, in which her hands were hidden! And her knees which outlined themselves under some checkered blue-green Scotch cloth! My God, is it possible to speak of it all in words? But the main thing, the main thing: what answer could one give to this declaration, so shattering by its unexpectedness, terror and happiness? Yes, what could one say to the expectant expression of this trustfully uplifted, pale face, somewhat altered from embarrassment or, possibly, from the effort at a smile?"

We were silent, also at a loss for what to say, how to answer these questions, and our perplexed eyes were fixed on the sparkling ones of our companion, whose face had grown red. And he answered his own questions:

"Nothing, nothing, simply nothing! There are moments when it is simply superfluous to give the slightest utterance. And, luckily—it is to the great credit of our traveler—he did not utter a single sound. And she comprehended his petrifaction, for she saw his face. After waiting for some time, motionless in that awkward and painful silence which followed on her terrible question, she rose and, removing a warm hand from the warm, fragrant muff, she embraced him round the neck and tenderly and passionately kissed him. It was one of those kisses which one remembers not alone on the death-bed but in the grave. Yes-s, that is all: she kissed him and—went away. And that is how the episode ended. . . .

"Well, enough about that!" suddenly the composer exclaimed, changing his voice, and with simulated cheerfulness loudly added: "And now, to celebrate the occasion, let us drink for all we are worth! Let us drink for all who love us, for all whom we idiots did not know how to appreciate, with whom we'd have been happy, blessed, from whom afterwards we had parted, losing ourselves in life for ever and ever, and still nevertheless for ever remained bound with the most terrible bond possible in this world! And I issue a warning: if any of you, by so much as a single word, adds to my recent narrative, I'll fling at his skull this very bottle of champagne. . . . Waiter!" he shouted, full throat, down the room, "where's that fish-soup! And fetch some sherry, sherry, a barrel of sherry, so I might plunge my phiz into it, horns and all!"

We prolonged our repast until eleven at night. Then we hired a cabby to take us to the cabaret-restaurant Yara, and from Yara we went to the Stryelna, where before dawn we ate *blini* * and drank vodka (you know the kind!), and generally conducted ourselves

---

* Pancakes.

shockingly: we sang, we shouted and even danced the *kazatchka.** The composer danced silently, fiercely and rapturously, with a lightness you would have scarcely expected from his figure. And a *troika* † winged us home in full daylight; it was a rosy, frosty morning. And when we swept past the Monastery of Our Lord's Passion, there loomed above the roofs the icy red sun, and from the belfry there came the first, peculiarly somber, superb stroke, shaking the whole of frosty Moscow, and the composer suddenly snatched off his cap and with all his might and with tears in his voice shouted across the square:

"Oh, sun! Oh, my beloved! Hurrah-h!"

* Cossack dance.
† Vehicle with team of three horses abreast.

METEOR

IT is Christmas, there is much snow, the days are
clear and frosty, the hackney sleighs are dashing along
friskily, invitingly; from two o'clock onward a military band is performing on the skating-rink in the city
park.

Three versts out of the city there is an old pine
grove.

A party of young men and women, students, laughing and chattering, are approaching it on long Swedish
skis, clasping in the right hand slender poles with a

kind of wheel at the lower end; the party consists of a male *lycée* student, a girl *gymnasium* student, a tall robust rich young man, a cadet, and a college girl with *pince-nez* who is nearsighted, awkward and rather touchy. Of all the party she alone is silent and makes her way more cautiously and more clumsily than the rest. She alone is attired in a proper skiing costume, in a white knitted sweater and a cap to match.

The grove looms nearer, gains in pictorial majesty, becomes blacker and greener. Above it is already visible the transparently pale moon. To the right the clear sun almost touches the edge of the far-reaching golden-radiant snowy plain with a scarcely noticeable greenish tone.

The college girl is advancing ahead of the others, stumbling at times and dropping her *pince-nez*. She is the first to enter the grove, through an immense opening between the mast-like pines. The skiing costume outlines her big rear and breasts. The animated, swarthy, broad-nosed cadet, every instant following close upon her heels, persists in mocking her, uttering jests at her expense. She does not allow a single remark of his to pass without replying with a spiteful ready wit, and goes on diligently plowing her way. Surely, there is something between them.

In the grove it is darkling, freezing; the high sky above the opening is colder, bluer; in the far fore-distance, beyond a glade, the tops of several particularly tall pines are glinting red. In the grove it is even sweeter to feel oneself young, in a holiday mood, every moment close to some sort of happiness, breathing in this winter, ethereal air. The *lycée* student feels his happiness more intensely than the others, as he moves the whole while by the side of the *gymnasium* girl.

More calm than the rest is the rich young man with his perpetual inordinately tender complexion, with his gentle, spotted aristocratic rosiness.

They pause in the glade, gaily resting there, all talking at once; the men smoke, getting particular enjoyment from the tobacco. They all have animated faces, shining eyes, and there are light particles of frost on their eye-lashes.

"Now where shall we go?"

"Below, of course, to the river!"

"What an idea, gentlemen! And you call yourselves skiers!"

"And who's this? I wonder if it's the Ilyins? What luck to run into them here!"

Numerous pathways between lofty pines stretch from the glade in all directions. From the pathway which leads directly from the river two figures are approaching, those of a man and a woman. The woman's laughter is audible, and it gives the impression of falsetto.

"Who is it?" asks the *lycée* student's *gymnasium* girl. "Your eye-sight is better than mine."

"They are your partners in amateur theatricals. Miss Zalyesskaya and Mr. Potemkin."

"Ah, but I haven't the least desire to meet them! I simply can't stand her. Let's go away somewhere. We'll meet our party in the meadow."

"At your service. . . . Ladies and gentlemen, we'll take our leave for a while. We'll see you soon on the river."

"What's the idea?" the cadet asks, awkwardly rolling his eyes. "What's the meaning of this sudden preposterous notion?"

"The time has come to explain our relations," said the *gymnasium* girl, laughing. "*Au revoir*, gentlemen. We leave you behind to envy us."

And, taking each other by the hand, the *lycée* student and the *gymnasium* girl glide on their skis along the path to the right. They are accompanied by outcries of farewell, and by quips.

The *lycée* student's heart is beating hard. He feels that, under the guise of a jest, with that tranquil and astonishing audacity of which only women are capable, she had spoken the truth. He knows that during these holiday times everything had been said without words between him and her, and that they had been waiting for the right moment and sufficient resolution definitely to establish that which had been said without words. And now this moment has suddenly come. She glides on, however, in silence, and his perturbation is increased by the doubt as to whether or not he had misinterpreted the meaning of her words.

She remains silent, and goes on gliding on her skis as if nothing had happened. And, owing to his perturbation, he is also silent, or else gives utterance to some perfectly fatuous remark.

"Would you prefer to turn to the left? The snow's deeper there. . . ."

"No, thanks, it's lovely right here. . . ."

And, resuming their silence, they glide along on their skis, their bodies slightly inclined forward. The surrounding snow, amidst the rosy pine trunks, steadily grows deeper, whiter, and the pines all the while snowier. The evening gently goes on changing the tints, gradually merging with the presently enthroned moonlit night.

"Oh, I think I'm quite tired now!" she says at last, turning to him her flushed face, faintly smiling. "Where are we going? I'm afraid we'll get lost. . . ."

His heart, even more than before, grows faint within him, but he tries to speak as normally as possible:

"Just a little farther. There'll be another glade soon, and a bench—don't you remember it? Only go more quietly, more evenly. Like this: one, two . . . one, two. . . ."

Once in the glade, near the bench, plunged in snow, he releases her hand, and, on releasing it, immediately feels what a delight it had been to hold it, concentrating—as it were—in itself the entire loveliness of her feminine being.

He stamps down the snow near the bench, and with one of the skis shapes a snow pillow out of it, brushing off the dry fragments of snow with his handkerchief. She sits down in the place thus made for her, and for a few moments closes her eyes in bliss.

"How lovely. How quiet it is here. . . . What sort of birds are these?"

Fat, goitrous, red-breasted bullfinches are flying from one juniper-bush to another.

"They are bullfinches."

"How handsome they are!"

"If you like, I'll kill one."

And he draws a small revolver from his pocket.

"No, it's not necessary," she says with an indecisive smile.

One fat bullfinch comes flying quite close to them.

"There, you see, he himself comes to meet death. . . . I'm going to shoot."

"No, no, it's not necessary."

"Are you afraid?"

"No, but I don't want to. . . ."

She makes a weak gesture with her hand in the direction of the bullfinch, but the bullfinch only comes flying nearer. And at that very instant, like the snapping of a whip, there is the sound of a discharge, from which in horror she shuts her eyes and puts her hands to her ears.

There is no longer any bullfinch on the bush. He must have missed it, of course! When again she lifts her eyes upward she sees that the moon is already among the tops of the pines and in its vicinity a soaring silvery hawk, frightened out of some hiding place by the shot. Then they search among the bushes. There, in a little tousled lump, lies the bullfinch upon the snow.

"It's perfectly incredible!" the *lycée* student exclaims, as he bends over it. "A little shot out of the revolver, and suddenly it's all over!"

At the same time he becomes even more intensely aware of time's passing, of their saying and doing the things not at all pertinent to the occasion.

"And haven't you any pity for it?" she asks, surveying the still warm bullfinch.

"Not a bit of it!" he jestingly replies with some effort, while his teeth chatter from inward tremors at the sight of her lips, the fur around her neck, the small shoes in the snow. "Why, you've soiled your hands in the blood. . . ."

She lays the bullfinch on the bench and raises up to her companion her eyes, which seem questioning and expectant.

"Allow me to wipe it off with snow. . . ."

She reaches out her hand to him. He wipes off the blood, while his heart grows faint with the almost intolerable desire to kiss her, to embrace her.

The evening passes. The moon among the pines now gleams like a mirror. In the light shadow flung by the tops of the pines the snow has taken on the color of ashes, while in the illumed places it sparkles with a jewel-like effulgence. The frost grows intenser.

"Anyhow, what are we doing here?" she says, suddenly rising. "We're running the risk of not finding them. Let's hurry!"

And again they take each other's hand and speed on their skis. Ten, fifteen minutes pass. . . .

"Stop! I don't think we're going in the right direction! Where are we? There's another glade of some sort. . . ."

"No. We're all right," says the *lycée* student. "Look —the glade slopes there. That's where it goes down to the river. We've been going all the time to the left, without noticing it."

Nevertheless, she remains standing, glancing round her, like one lost. Above their heads the moon now shines in a nocturnal mood; the shadows among the pines are black, palpable; on the edge of the glade a black hut without windows stands plunged in snow-drifts; its snowy, swollen roof is all aglitter with white and blue diamonds. Dead silence everywhere.

"You've led me astray somewhere," she says in a low voice, this time with real fear. "Let's go back!"

But he looks strangely at her, and pulls her forward by the hand.

"Let's just look into this hut. . . . For only a minute or so. . . ."

She advances several paces, but near the hut she resolutely resists, stopping and removing her hand from his. He, flinging his skis aside, goes upon a hardened drift toward the open door and, bending down, hides in the darkness of the hut. A few moments pass, and his voice resounds from the hut:

"It's simply lovely here! Just glance through the window, if you don't want to come in! Surely you're not afraid?"

"No, I don't want to. Where are you? Let's go! It's getting late."

"How lovely the moonlight is in here! It is something fabulous!"

"If you don't come out, I'll go away alone. . . ."

And, her feet crunching upon the frosty snow, she walks up to the window, and glances in:

"Where are you?"

And suddenly she is blinded by such a wonderful, such a terrible and paradisiacally beautiful green light from a meteor cutting across the whole sky and bursting, that she gives a scream and in terror runs through the open door of the hut. . . .

In the course of half an hour they again go out into the moonlit glade and pursue their way toward the river, and though they hear the calls made to them they are incapable of uttering a single word.

A NIGHT AT SEA

THE steamer from Odessa bound for the Caucasus,
stopped at night at Eupatoria.

A downright Hades ensued on and around the
steamer. The capstans rattled, a fierce clamor rose from
those who received the cargo as well as from those
who delivered it from the immense barge below; with
shouting and wrangling the passengers' ladder was
lowered and, with incomprehensibly fierce haste, as if
they were rushing to an assault, the Oriental rabble
bearing their chattels surged upward; the little electric

lamp, hanging above the platform of the ladder, cast a sharp glare on the dense disorderly troop of dirty fezes and turbans projecting from cowls, on bulging eyes, on shoulders pushing forward, on hands feverishly clutching the hand-rail; there were groans below, near the lower steps, which were repeatedly submerged by the waves; there also they wrangled and shouted, fell back and grappled; oars beat upon the water, row-boats filled with humanity collided with one another—now they rose upon a wave, now fell precipitately, or disappeared from the ship's side into the darkness. And all the while the dolphin-like shape of the steamer, flexibly, as though on an elastic, heaved now to one side now to the other. . . .

At last things began to quiet down.

A very erect gentleman, with erect shoulders, among the last to come aboard, handed the steward standing near the first-class deck-cabin his ticket and bag and, on discovering that there was no vacant berth, walked toward the stern. It was dark here, several canvas deck-chairs were scattered about the deck, and in one of them a half-recumbent figure was darkly outlined, wrapped in plaid. The new passenger chose a place a few feet away from him. The deck-chair was low and when he dropped into it the canvas stretched and formed a very comfortable and pleasant shelter. The ship rose and fell, slowly yielding to the rhythm of the waves. The soft breeze of a summer night blew, faintly redolent of the sea. The simple, peaceful summer night, with a clear sky full of modest petty stars, gave out a soft pellucid darkness. The remote lights were pale and because of the lateness of the hour seemed somnolent. Soon everything on the ship resumed its order, calm commanding voices were heard, the anchor chain rattled. . . . Then the stern trembled, the propellers and the waters sounded. The lights of the distant shore, low and widely scattered, began to recede. The ship stopped rocking. . . .

Both passengers gave the appearance of being asleep, so motionlessly did they recline in their chairs. But no, they were not asleep, but were regarding each other with a peculiar intentness in that half-darkness. At last, the first passenger, he whose legs were covered with the plaid rug, asked simply and calmly:

"You also bound for the Crimea?"

The second passenger, with the erect shoulders, without the least hurry, answered in the same voice:

"Yes, for the Crimea—and farther. I'll make a stop-over in Alupka, then go on to Hagra."

"I recognized you at once," said the first passenger.

"And I you," replied the second.

"A strange and unexpected meeting!"

"Could scarcely be more so."

"Strictly speaking, it isn't merely that I recognized

you. I had indeed a sort of premonition, unaccountable if you like, that you must appear. So it was not a matter of recognition at all."

"Curious. I experienced the same thing."

"Really? That's very strange. It seems that there are such moments in life—shall we call them extraordinary? Life, perhaps, is not as simple as it sometimes appears."

"Perhaps. But then another thing is possible: that you and I have simply imagined the feelings of this moment instead of having a premonition."

"Perhaps. That's very possible. Yes, it must be so."

"There you see. We reason this way and that, but life is perhaps more simple. More like the rabble which crowded the ladder. What made the fools hurry the way they did, and trample upon one another?"

The two companions lapsed into a brief silence. Then they resumed.

"How long is it since we've met? Twenty-three years, isn't it?" the first passenger, reposing under the plaid rug, asked.

"Yes, just about," replied the other. "It will be exactly twenty-three years this autumn. You and I can easily figure that out. And it's almost a quarter of a century!"

"A long time. A whole life. That's to say, your life and mine are practically over."

"Quite, quite. What of that? Does that terrify you?"

"H'm! Of course not. Almost not at all. To be sure, it's sheer nonsense to call it terrifying, that is when we try to frighten ourselves by saying, 'Dear fellow, your life's over! In ten years or so you'll have to lie in a grave!' Just think of it, in a grave! That's not a joke."

"Quite. But I'll go farther than that. You know, of course, that I am something of a celebrity in the medical world?"

"Who doesn't know it? Of course, I know. And that your humble servant is also a celebrity, are you aware of that?"

"Naturally. It's possible for me to confess that I'm an admirer of yours."

"So, so, we're both celebrities.—But you were about to say something?"

"Merely this, that thanks to my celebrity, that is to certain knowledge, heaven knows it's no great wisdom, but certainly definite enough for all purposes, I know with fair certainty that far from having ten years of life left I haven't that many months. Well, at the very most—a year. I have personally established—and I am supported in my knowledge by my medical colleagues—that I am suffering from a mortal disease. I assure you, I go on behaving as if nothing had hap-

53

pened. All I do is to indulge in sarcastic smiles: 'Dear fellow, you've wanted to surpass everyone in the knowledge of all sorts of causes of death, in order to crow and live magnificently, but instead what's happened to you—you've made the magnificent discovery of your own approaching death!' I might have been deceived, made a fool of—'What are you saying, dear old chap, there's still a lot of sap left in the old bones!' —but they can't fool me, they can't feed me a pack of lies! It's stupid and awkward. So awkward in fact that they've taken to oversalting the dish out of frankness, mixed up with feeling and flattery: 'Well, esteemed colleague, we won't try to fool you. . . . *Finita la comedia!*' "

"Are you in earnest?" the first passenger asked.

"Quite in earnest," the second answered. "But what's the main thing? I know of a chap who is mortal, ergo I too must die, but when will that happen to him? But here, unfortunately, is quite another matter: it won't happen merely sometime, but within a year. And is a year a lot of time? During the coming summer you'll be traveling somewhere on the blue ocean, while in Moscow, in the graveyard of the Holy Virgin, my honored bones will lie underground. Well, what of it? Actually, I experience no feeling of any kind at the thought. Worse still, no one appears to see any kind of courage in this, not even the students when I describe to them my disease and its course as something interesting from the clinical point of view, which I am able to do because of my own idiotic unfeelingness. Not even those who work with me and know my fatal secret are moved by it. Take yourself, for example—do you feel terrified at all on my account?".

"Do I feel terrified on your account? I must confess, no. Actually, not at all."

"And, of course, you don't feel at all sorry for me?"

"No, nor sorry. And I venture to say that you have no belief whatsoever in those blessed places, in which there is neither grief nor affliction, but only paradisial apples?""

"What sort of faith can you and I have?"

And again both lapsed into silence. Then they took out cigars and began to smoke.

"Just make a note of it," said the first passenger, the one who lay under his plaid rug, "neither of us is showing off now, neither is playing a part before the other, as before an imaginary listener. We both of us are, in truth, speaking quite simply and without premeditated cynicism, without any spiteful boast, in which nevertheless there is always some sort of compensation; now, let us glance at the position in which we find ourselves. We are conversing simply and grow silent without the least significance, without the least stoical wisdom. Generally speaking, there is no more sensual animal on earth than a human being, the cunning human soul is capable of extracting self-gratification from everything. But I don't see even this in the episode which involves me with you. It is all the more curious because it is necessary to add to our, as you express yourself, idiotic unfeelingness the whole peculiarity of our mutual relations. For, after all, there is a terribly close bond between us. That is, to speak more precisely, there should have been a bond between us."

"There's no gainsaying that!" replied the other. "Of course, I have brought horror into your life. I imagine that you've survived it."

"Yes, and even more than you can imagine. And, generally speaking, it is horrible, that whole nightmare which is experienced by the male, lover, husband, whose wife has been taken, enticed away from him, and who for nights and days, almost ceaselessly, every instant, shrinks from the agonies of wounded self-love, from the terrible jealous fancies about the happiness experienced by his rival, and from the hopeless, perpetually thwarted tenderness—to be more precise, sexual emotion—toward the lost female, whom, at one and the same time, he desires to throttle in the most ferocious hatred and to shower upon the most humiliating tokens of truly canine submissiveness and devotion. This, in general, is unutterably horrible. Add to this

the fact that I'm by no means an ordinary human being, but an individual with a heightened consciousness,
with a heightened imagination. Now you can surmise
what I have undergone in the course of years."

"Not years, surely?"

"I assure you, not less than three years. Yes, and
even later the mere thought of you and of her, of
your intimacy with her, would scorch me as with a red-
hot iron. That's comprehensible too. Well, to rob a
man of his bride-to-be, that's one thing. But to seduce
a man's mistress or, as in my case, a man's wife! She,
you must remember, with whom you slept—pardon my
bluntness—was known to me in all the peculiarities of
body and soul like the five fingers of my own hand!
Just think what scope it gives to the jealous imagination. How is one to survive the knowledge of her
domination by another? It is all simply beyond human endurance. Can you wonder then that I nearly
drank myself to death, that I lost my health, my will?
That I lost the prime development of my strength, of
my gifts? I can say, without exaggeration, that you
simply broke me in two. I've grown together, of
course, but what was the sense of it? In any case, little
was left of my former self, and it couldn't have been
otherwise. For you'd broken into the holy of the holies
of my existence! Prince Gautam, in choosing for himself a bride and on seeing Yasodkhara, who had 'the

form of a goddess and the eyes of a doe in spring,' was so stirred by her that he raised the very devil of a mess in competition with the other youths—he shot from his bow, for example, so that it was audible for seven thousand miles—then he removed his necklace of precious gems, and, putting it on Yasodkhara, said: 'I chose her because we played together in the woods in ages long gone by, when I was the son of a huntsman and she a maid of the woods: my soul suddenly remembered her!' She had on that day a black-golden mantle, and the Prince glanced at her and said: 'She's wearing a black-golden mantle because myriads of years ago, when I was a huntsman, I saw her in the woods in the shape of a panther: and my soul has suddenly remembered her!' You'll forgive me for indulging in all this poetry, but there is a great and terrible truth in it. Just try to penetrate into the meaning of these astonishing words! I am referring to the suddenly awakened memory and to the horror which occurs when this most sacred of meetings in the world is violated by a stranger. Who knows—I might have also shot so it would have been audible for thousands of miles. Then—suddenly—you appeared. . . ."

"Well, and how do you feel toward me now?" asked the gentleman with the erect shoulders. "Spite? Repugnance? A thirst for vengeance?"

"Just think of it: simply nothing! Notwithstanding

your tirade, simply nothing. Horror, horror. There's your 'my soul suddenly remembered'! But you know that well yourself, I mean that I feel nothing. Otherwise, you'd not have asked."

"You're quite right. I know. And that too is very terrifying."

"All the same, we're not a bit terrified. The whole horror consists in that we're not a bit terrified."

"Yes, that's it. Not a bit. Men say there's a past! That's all nonsense. Strictly speaking, human beings have no past. Only, perhaps, they catch a faint echo of something experienced at one time. . . ."

And once more a silence fell upon the two men. The steamer trembled, went on; with a measured rhythm rose and fell the soft din of the drowsy wave which came alongside; rapidly, monotonously, behind the monotonously sounding stern, revolved the logline, now and then giving vent to a slight, mysterious ringing sound: dzin-n. . . . Then the passenger with the erect shoulders asked:

"Well, tell me. . . . What did you feel when you heard of her death? Did you feel anything?"

"No, almost nothing," answered the passenger under the plaid rug. "I only felt a certain astonishment at my unfeelingness. I opened a newspaper in the morning, and there lightly struck my eye: 'By God's will, etc., etc. . . .' Because one is unaccustomed to it, it is strange to see the name of someone familiar and close to you in that black frame, in that fatal place in the newspaper, printed so solemnly, in large type. . . . Well, I did try to mourn. But, old chap, wasn't she the same who . . . But—

"From indifferent lips I heard the news of death
And indifferently I hearkened. . . .

"Even grief was lacking. There was only some sort of weak pity. . . . Yet was she not the same whom 'my soul suddenly remembered'? Was she not my first, and such an intense love of many years? I became acquainted with her at the time of her greatest loveliness, innocence and that almost adolescent trustfulness and timidity which agitates a male heart unspeakably, because perhaps there must be in all femininity this trusting helplessness, something childlike, the token that the girl, the woman, always keeps hidden within her the as yet unborn babe. And there it was, to me first, in a sort of divine bliss and terror, she truly yielded everything God gave her. Truly a million times, in such rapture as I had not known before or since, I kissed her maiden body, the most beautiful thing on earth. And was it not for her that literally night and day for years I nearly went out of my mind? It was for her that I wept, tore my hair, tried suicide, drank, vented my spite, fiercely destroyed what was probably my most precious labor. . . . Well, twenty years pass by—and I stupidly gaze at her name in the mourning frame, stupidly I imagine her in her grave. . . . I imagine something unpleasant, nothing more. I assure you, that is the truth. What about yourself—I'm referring to the present—do you feel anything?"

"I? I can't say I do. What's the good of hiding the fact? To be sure, scarcely a thing. . . ."

The steamer continued its way; with a hissing sound there rose before us wave upon wave, approaching with a clamor and dashing against the ship's side; monotonously dinned and seethed the snow-white path stretching behind the stern. A soft breeze blew, the starry design remained motionless in the heights, above the black funnel, above the rigging, above the slender point of the fore-mast. . . .

"Do you know what?" suddenly said the first passenger, as if suddenly awakened. "Do you know what the main thing is? It is, that I could not in any way connect her, the one who had died, with that other, about whom I have just spoken to you. Not in any way. Absolutely in no way. She, the other, was quite separate. And to say that I felt nothing at all toward her, the other, would be an absolute lie. So I have not spoken the truth. It's not at all like that."

The other reflected.

"Well, and what then?"

"Simply this, that most of our conversation has been without point."

"Oh, without point?" said the passenger with the erect shoulders. "She, the other, as you express yourself, is simply you, your imagination, your feelings—in short, something your own. And that means you've stirred and tormented yourself wholly with yourself. Consider that well."

"Do you think so? I don't know. Maybe. . . . Yes, it's possible. . . ."

"Yes, and did you long torment yourself with yourself? Ten minutes. Well, let's say half an hour. Even a whole day."

"Yes, yes. It's terrible, but you may be right. And where is she now? There perhaps, in this lovely sky?"

"Allah alone knows, my friend. Most likely, nowhere."

"Do you think so? Yes, yes. . . . Most likely, it is so. . . ."

The open flat sea in an almost black circle lay under the luminous cupola of the nocturnal sky. And lost in this round darkening plain the tiny steamer stolidly and unswervingly pursued its path. And endlessly there stretched behind it the drowsily seething pale-milken way—there, into the distance, where the nocturnal sky merged with the sea, where the horizon, in

contrast to this milkiness, appeared dark and sorrow-
ful. And the log-line went on revolving and revolving
and mysteriously something at moments ticked off, and
gave vent to a slender ringing sound: dzi-in-n. . . .

After a silence, the two men, in low voices, said
simply to each other:

"Good night."

"Good night."

AN UNKNOWN FRIEND

October 7, 19 . . .

U PON this picture post-card with its sad and majestic view of a moonlit night on the shores of the Atlantic Ocean I make haste to write you my ardent gratitude for your last book. These shores are my second Fatherland, they are the last frontier of the European domains of Great Britain—so you can see from what a distance one of your unknown friends sends you a greeting. May you be happy, and may God preserve you.

October 8.

Here is still another view of that desolate land, whither the fates have cast me for ever.

Yesterday, while it rained terribly—we have perpetual rain here—I went to town on business and quite by chance bought your book and read it without interruption on my return journey to our villa where we live the year round for the sake of my health. Owing to the rain and the clouds it was quite dark, the flowers and the verdure in the gardens appeared unusually bright, the empty tram-car went along speedily, emitting violet flashes, while I read and read and, incomprehensibly, felt almost rapturously happy.

Good-bye. Once more I thank you. I have a strong desire to say something else, but what? I do not know. I cannot define my feelings.

October 10.

Again I feel strongly impelled to write to you. I have an idea that you receive a good many letters like mine. But aren't these letters responses of precisely those human souls for whom you are creating? Then why should I remain silent? You were the one to begin communicating with me by allowing your book to go out into the world, a book addressed to me as to others. . . .

The rain has been pouring the entire day upon our almost unnaturally green garden, and since early morning an uncheerful fire has been flaring in the fire-place. I was moved by a desire to speak to you, and I had so much to say to you, but you know better than others how difficult it is, how almost impossible—to unburden oneself. I am still under the impression of something incomprehensible and enigmatic, yet something inexpressibly lovely, which I owe to you—please explain to me what it means, this mood. In general, is it something which human beings experience in their reaction to art? Is it the enchantment which comes from human skill, human power? The awakened desire for personal happiness, which always, unquenchably, lives in us and revives particularly under the influence of something acting on our feelings—of music, poetry, some sort of reminiscent images, some sort of odor? Or is it the joy of the perception of the beauty of the human soul, revealed to us by the rare few, like yourself, reminding us that, in spite of everything, this divine beauty does exist? Here I happen to read something—sometimes even something full of terror—and I suddenly say to myself: "Oh God, how beautiful this is!"

Farewell, soon I will write you again. I have an idea

that there is nothing wrong in this. It seems to be accepted—that readers should write to authors. Quite apart from that, it is more than likely that you don't even read my letters . . . though, to be sure, the thought saddens me.

The same night.

Forgive me, it may sound stupid to you, but I can't help saying: I'm not young, I have a fifteen-year-old daughter, quite a young lady in fact, but I was not so bad-looking at one time, and I haven't changed awfully much. . . . All the same, I don't want you to imagine me other than as I actually am.

October 11.

Sheer necessity has forced me to share with you the perturbation into which your genius has flung me, reacting upon me like a sad if exalted music. Why should I feel this necessity to share it with you? I don't know, nor do you, but we both know that this necessity of the human heart is not to be rooted out, that without it there is no life, and that in it is some great mystery. You yourself know that you write from sheer necessity and that moreover—you surrender your whole self to it.

I have always been a persistent reader—and I have

written quite a few diaries, as do all persons not fully satisfied with life. To this day I read a great deal. I have also read some of your writings, not many, though I always knew you chiefly by name. And then, suddenly, I come upon your new book. . . . How strange it is! Someone's pen, in some remote place, has written something; someone's soul has expressed a tiny fragment of its secret life in slight insinuations—what power there is in the word, even such as yours!—and suddenly space and time vanish, differences in fate and circumstance disappear, and your thoughts and feelings become mine, our common possession. Truly, there is but one, but a single soul in this world. After this, is not my overpowering impulse to write you an understandable one? Is it not understandable why I should want to express myself, share something with you, give vent to my unhappy thoughts? Are not your writings the very same thing as my letters to you? Do you not yourself confess something to someone, send out your lines to some unknown stranger into some remote space? You too give vent to your unhappy thoughts, mostly to unhappy thoughts, because your plaint, if expressed in different words, is a prayer for sympathy, inseparable from a human being: how much there is of it in songs, in prayers, in verses, in outpourings of love!

Perhaps, you will deign me a reply, if but two words? Please answer!

October 13.

Again it is night, and I write to you, in my bedroom, tormented by an incomprehensible desire to say something, which may sound naïve, but which in any case will not express that which one feels. And, actually, I haven't so much to say: only that I feel so very sad, and am sorry for myself—but that I am, nevertheless, very happy in my sadness and self-pity. It is sad for me to think that I am somewhere in an alien land, on the most extreme western shores of Europe, in a suburban villa, in the midst of autumnal darkness and sea fog, which stretches straight across to America itself. It is sad for me to think that I am alone not only in this lovely and comfortable room but in the whole world. Above all, it is sad to reflect that you, whom I have invented and from whom I seem to be awaiting something, should be so infinitely remote from me and so unknown to me and, of course, notwithstanding what I have said, so alien to me and so correct in this. . . .

Actually, everything in the world is lovely, even this shaded lamp and the golden light it casts, and the sparkling white on my opened bed, and my dressing-gown, my foot in the slipper and my lean arm in the broad sleeve. And a great pity wells up in me concerning everything: to what purpose is it all? Everything passes, yes, everything will pass, and everything is vain, even as my eternal expectation of something, which might alter my life. . . .

I entreat of you—write to me. Naturally, a mere two or three words, if only that I might know that you are listening to me. Forgive my persistence.

October 15.

This is our city, our cathedral. The deserted cliff coast—of my first post-card to you—is somewhat farther, more north. But this city, and its cathedral—everything is stern, gloomy here. Granite, slate, asphalt, and rain, rain. . . .

Yes, write me briefly. I understand very well that you have nothing to say to me, except for two or three words, and, believe me, I'll not take it amiss. But write to me, write to me!

October 21.

Alas, there is no letter from you. Yet fifteen days have passed since I first wrote to you. . . .

It is possible, of course, that your publisher has not yet forwarded my letters. Or it is possible that pressing occupations are taking up your time, or it may be social engagements. It is very sad for me to think this, but it is better to assume that such is the case than to imagine

73

that you have simply ignored my request. To think so is both very painful and humiliating. You will say that I have no right whatsoever to your consideration and that therefore there can be no question of pain or humiliation. But is it really true that I do not possess this right? It may be that I have this right, once I have experienced certain feelings toward you. Really, can you name even a single Romeo who did not demand reciprocal emotions even without the least justification; or an Othello who was jealous because he had a right to be? One and the other says: once I love, is it possible not to return my love—and is it possible to betray me? This is no simple wish that I may be loved, it is something far more complex, something greater. Once I love something or someone, it is already mine, and is within me. . . . In any case, I am incapable of explaining it to you as it should be explained; I only know that thus it has always seemed to people and always will; and I feel that some very deep truth is hidden here. Everything is fabulous, everything is incomprehensible in this world. . . .

However it may be, there is no response from you, and I am writing again. Inexplicably, the thought has come to me, that you are in some way near to me—is it, really, so unreasonable a thought?—and I have come to believe this thought of mine and have persisted in writing to you, and I already know that the oftener I write to you the more necessary it will be to continue, because stronger and stronger will become the bond between you and me. I do not paint a picture of you in my mind, I see not at all your physical features. To whom, then, am I writing? To myself? It does not really matter. For I too am—you.

Still—I entreat a response!

October 22.

It is a marvelous day, there is a lightness in my soul, the windows are open, and the sun and the warm air make one think of spring. A strange land this! In the summer it rains and is cold, in the autumn and winter it rains and is warm, but at times such perfect days fall out as to make you wonder: is it really winter or is it the Italian spring? Oh, Italy, Italy when I was still eighteen, with all my hopes, my exultant trustfulness, my anticipations on the threshold of life, which was yet all before me and all in a sun-mist, like the hills, the valleys and blooming gardens surrounding Vesuvius! Forgive me, I know that this is far from being new, but what of it?

The same night.

It is possible that you have not written me because I may seem to you of too abstract a nature. Allow me, then, to present you with a few more facts about my life. Already sixteen years have passed since my marriage. My husband is a Frenchman. I made his acquaintance one winter on the French Riviera, we were married in Rome, and after a honeymoon in Italy we settled here for ever. I have three children, a boy and two girls. Do I love them? Yes, yet not altogether as mothers so often love their children, seeing their whole life in their family, in their children. As long as they were small, I constantly looked after them, shared in their play and occupations, but now they have little need of me, and I have plenty of leisure, which I employ in reading. My own kin are far from me, our ways in life have parted, and we have so few interests in common that a correspondence between us is very rare. In connection with my husband's interests, it is often necessary for me to see people, to pay and receive visits, to be present at evening parties and at dinners. But I have no intimate friends or companions. I am very little like the native ladies, and I have no faith in friendship between men and women. . . .

But enough about me. If you reply, will you at least say a few words about yourself? The sort of being you are. Where your permanent home is. Whether you love Shakespeare or Shelley, Goethe or Dante, Balzac or Flaubert. Whether you love music, and what your favorite pieces are. Whether married, or not. Whether already tied in a bond grown irksome, or whether you have a bride in that still tender, lovely time, when everything is new and gay, before there are memories, which only torment and deceive, hinting at a happiness, elusive and wasted?

Please write me, if you only can!

November 1.

Still no letter from you. What a torture! Such a torture, that I sometimes curse the day and hour when I resolved to write to you. . . .

The worst thing about it is that there is no way out of the situation. No matter how much I have tried to assure myself that there would be no letter, that it was useless to expect one, I nevertheless wait: for who can guarantee that it will actually fail to come? Oh, if I only really knew that you would not write! I would then be happy. But no, no, it is better to live in hope. I hope, I wait!

November 3.

There is no letter, and my torments continue. . . . The morning hours are the most difficult. It is then

77

that, with an unnatural calm and with hands cold from inward perturbation, I lingeringly dress, proceed to my coffee, pass a musical hour with my daughter, who studies her lesson with such touching diligence and sits at the piano so erect, so attractively erect, as only young girls can in their fifteenth year. At last at mid-day the post arrives, and I rush toward it, only to find nothing —and I almost grow calm until the following morning. . . .

Again it is a perfect day. The low sun is clear and benign. There are many bare, dark trees in the garden; the autumn flowers are in bloom. And there is something ethereal, blue, incredibly lovely in the valleys, beyond the branches of the garden. And the heart is possessed with gratitude to someone and for some thing. For what? There is really nothing and nothing will happen . . . although is this true, is it correct to say there's nothing when it is actually here—this gratitude charming the soul?

I thank you also for giving me the possibility of inventing you. You will never recognize me, never meet me, but in this there is much melancholy beauty. And, perhaps, it is just as well that you have not written me a single word and that I have not met you in the flesh. For could I have spoken with you and felt you as I feel you now if I knew you or even if I had but a single letter from you? Undoubtedly you would not have been the same, undoubtedly a little worse than I have imagined you, and I'd have found some constraint in writing to you. . . .

It is growing cool, and still I am keeping the windows open, and still I am looking out into the gossamery blue veil stretching across the hollows and hillocks beyond the garden. And this blue is agonizingly beautiful, agonizingly because it is absolutely necessary to do something with it. But do what? I don't know. We do not know anything!

November 5.

This resembles a diary, but it is not at all a diary, because I now have a reader, even if it is a conjectured one. . . .

What impels you to write? A desire to recount something or to express yourself (even if but allegorically)? The latter, of course. Nine writers out of ten, even the famous ones, are mere tale-tellers; that is to say, their work essentially has nothing in common with what may be worthily called art. Then what is art? It is the prayer, the music, the song of the human soul. . . . Ah, if only I could leave behind me a few lines to say that I have lived, loved, rejoiced, that I once had youth, spring, Italy . . . that there is a remote land on the shores of the Atlantic, where I now live, love and even yet await something . . . that this ocean contains some miserable wild isles and the miserable wild life of human beings alien to the rest of the world, human beings whose origin, obscure language and purpose of existence no one knows and no one ever will know. . . .

Nevertheless, I am waiting, waiting for a letter. It's become a tiresome notion, a sort of spiritual illness.

November 7.

Yes, everything is fabulous. Of a letter there is, of course, not the slightest sign. And just think of it: because there's no such letter, there's no response from the human being whom I've never seen and never shall see, there's no answering call to my voice flung somewhere into the remote distance, into my dream, and I am lost in a mood of terrible loneliness, and am obsessed with a feeling of the terrible emptiness of the world. How empty, how empty!

And again rain, fog, dreariness. It is well that this is usual, as it should be. It has a calming effect on me.

Farewell, and may God forgive you for your hardness. Yes, it may be almost called that.

November 8.

It is only three o'clock in the afternoon, yet it is almost twilight from the mist and the rain.

And at five I shall have people to tea.

They'll arrive in the rain, by car, from the gloomy town, which during the rain shows even blacker with its black wet asphalt, its black wet roofs and black granite cathedral, whose spire is lost in the rain and the dusk. . . .

I am already dressed and am waiting, as it were, for my entrance on the stage. I am waiting for the moment when I shall speak as is expected of me, be pleasant, animated, courteous and just a little pale, which may so easily be accounted for by the weather. And, dressed as I am, I seem younger, feel myself to be the elder sister of my daughter and am ready to cry any moment. But really, I have lived through something strange, akin to love. For whom? How?

Farewell, I no longer expect anything—I say this quite frankly and firmly.

November 10.

Farewell, my unknown friend. I shall end my unanswered letters as I began them—with gratitude. I thank you for remaining unresponsive. It would have been worse otherwise. What could you have said to me? And how could we, without suffering embarrassment, have interrupted our correspondence? And what could I have said to you beside what I have already said? I have nothing more to say—I have said everything.

Actually, it is possible to write a mere two or three lines about any human life. Oh, yes. A mere two or three lines.

With a strange feeling—as if I had lost someone—as before I remain alone, with my house, with the nearness of the misty ocean, with the autumnal and winter dreariness. And again I shall return to my tranquil diary, the strange necessity for which, as for your writings, the heavens alone can explain.

Some days ago I saw you in a dream. You were somehow strange, taciturn, and you sat in the corner of a dark room and were invisible. Nevertheless, I saw you. But even in my dream I felt: how was it possible to see in a dream someone whom you haven't seen in life? Apparently God alone can create out of nothing. And I suffered agony, and I awoke in terror, and felt heavily oppressed.

Within another fifteen or twenty years, it is likely that there will be neither you nor me in this world. Until we meet in the next! Who knows for certain that it doesn't exist? Why, we scarcely understand our own dreams, the creations of our own imagination. Is it ours, this imagination, that is, to speak more precisely, what we call our imagination, our inventions, our dreams? Do we submit to our own will, when we aspire to this or that soul, as I aspire to yours?

Farewell. Or no, until we meet.

STRONGER THAN
DEATH

DEATH, where is thy sting? Let us recall what She, who was more beautiful than the sun, said to him in that self-same night, when they delivered up Her body to the grave: 'Don't weep for me, for, because of death, my days have become eternal; in the celestial world have my eyes opened for ever, while here on the mortal couch they seemed always to close. . . .'

"In the summer of the year one thousand three hundred and twenty-six of our Lord, the Signor Francesco Petrarch arrived in the city of Avignon in Provence, among the many others who followed the most Sacred Throne into exile. A year later it happened that he met on the path of his young life the Donna Laura and conceived a great love for her, which likened her to the image of Beatrice and the most renowned women of the earth. In that year, on the sixth day of April, on Friday of Passion-week, he listened to the morning service in the Church of Sainte-Claire, in Avignon; and it was then, when he had stayed out the service, and issued from the church on to the square, that glancing at others who were leaving the church he suddenly saw Donna Laura, daughter of the Knight Audibert, the young wife of Signor Ugo, whose worthy but commonplace image has not been preserved for posterity. . . ."

He saw her at the very moment when she appeared within the portals of the church.

"That spring was the twenty-third in his life, in Hers—the twentieth. And, if he possessed all the beauty natural to his young years, an ardent heart and nobility of blood, then Her youthful loveliness might be called heavenly. Blessed were those who saw her in life! She walked with eye-lashes, black as ebony, lowered; when she raised them, the sun-like radiance of Her glance left him amazed for eternity. . . ."

Thus he himself spoke of it more than once:

"It happened in the year one thousand three hundred and twenty-seven of our Lord, on the sixth day of the month of April. . . ."

This day was gloomy and rainy, one of those days by no means rare during the early spring in Avignon. It happened at a time which is now called ancient and in which everything seems beautiful: spring's inclemency, and the old stone city darkling under the rains, all its walls, churches, turrets, and all the human beings which once inhabited it, and their whole life, their whole existence, all their affairs and feelings. . . . He says:

"It happened in the hour of the crucifixion of our Lord Jesus, when the sun itself is invested with a sackcloth of grief. . . ."

On the pages of Virgil, his favorite book, from which he never parted and which always lay at the head of his bed, he wrote in his old age:

"Laura, renowned for her own virtues and celebrated by me, first rose before my eyes during my youth, in the year one thousand three hundred and twenty-seven of our Lord, on the sixth day of the month of April, in Avignon; in that same Avignon, in the same month of April, on the same sixth day, in that self-same hour, in the year one thousand three hundred and forty-eight, was extinguished the pure light of her life, during a time when chance brought me to Verona, alas, without knowledge of the fate which had overtaken me: it was not before I reached Parma did the fatal tidings come to me, in the same year, on the nineteenth day of May, in the morning. Her beautiful, chaste body was delivered up unto the earth in the tomb of the Menorite brothers, in the evening of the day of her death; and Her soul, I believe, returned to Heaven, its fatherland. In order the better to preserve the memory of this hour, I find it a bitter comfort to have made a note of it in the book which is ever before me: it was needful for me to possess myself of this hard knowledge, that henceforth there would not be anything any more to console me on the earth. It is for me to forsake its Babylon. By God's mercy, this will not be hard for me, bearing in mind the futile cares, the vain hopes and the sad issues of my ebbing life. . . ."

It has been recorded that in his youth he was strong, skilful; his head was small, round and firm of shape; his nose moderate, sensitive; the oval of his face, soft and precise; the flush of his cheeks gentle but healthy; the color of his eyes brown; his glance alert and ardent. "Already he was famed for his high gifts, his mind, the wealth of his knowledge and unwearying labors. Already he was haunted by that immeasurable love, which made his name immorta[1]. Withal, he participated in all the affairs of his age, devoted his genius to the creation of all its finest movements; in society he was distinguished for his disposition toward his fellow beings, the charm of his association with them, the eloquence of his speech in conversation. . . ."

The portrait in Avignon represents him in ripe years: as he was crowned by the monastery as the greatest man of his time; it is a noble Florentine profile, the whole aspect suggesting abundance of thought and life.

In his old age he wrote:

"I no longer think of anything but of Her: let her then hasten our meeting in heaven, for she draws and calls me to her!"

But he wrote instead in a letter to a friend:

"I desire that death should surprise me at work on a book, pen in hand, or, still better, if it please God, in tears at prayer. Keep well and happy. Live in courage and good spirits, as becomes a man!"

Several months after writing this letter, on June 20, 1374, his birthday, while sitting at work, he "suddenly fell forward, his head sinking on to his writings: Death had fulfilled his hopes. . . ."

In this also was "this consummation between earth and heaven."

The day on which they first saw each other was a day fated for her as well:

"Her heart was also passionate and tender; but scarcely less inflexible in duty and honor, in faith in God and His laws!

"My sovereign, she walked past me, solitarily resting in sweet thoughts of my love for Her. In order to greet Her, I rose, humbly bowing before her my paled brow. I was all a-tremble; She continued her way, after conferring upon me a few gracious words. . . ."

For twenty years he celebrated Laura's terrestrial image; for another quarter of a century—her image beyond the grave. He made a calculation that during all his life he had seen her, in a general way, less than a year; and, even then, always among other persons and always "invested with a dignified demeanor." But he also remembered something quite different:

"And once She did grow pale. It happened in the moment of my departure. She bowed low her divine face, and it seemed as if her silence spoke: why am I being forsaken by my faithful friend?"

Outwardly he experienced the joys and sorrows of simple mortals; he was not without a woman's love, a mortal, simple love, which hindered not the other, the "immortal" one, and he even had two children. She also had children; she was a faithful, worthy spouse. "But all through life Her soul awaited deliverance beyond the grave—for the love She bore the Other. . . ."

The black plague of 1348, which within a few weeks had counted sixty thousand victims in Avignon, also took her. And that same evening, in the light of resin torches, whose tempestuous crackling flames "banished infection," human beings attired in loose, wide, black smocks, with slits only for the eyes, buried Her in the spot which but three days before death she had graced with Her presence. That night Her soul, freed at last "for the love She bore the Other," made haste to keep the first tryst with him:

"The night which followed this ill-omened day, when the star shining in my life was extinguished, or, to be more accurate, again resumed its place in the heavens, that night began to yield its place to Aurora, when lo, a certain Beauty, even as perfect as Her earthly image, crowned with the most precious jewels of the East, rose before me. And, gently sighing, gave me the hand so long desired by me: Know, she said, know her, who had for always stepped into your path from the day of her first meeting with you; know, that for a lofty soul death is but a release from prison, that she frightens only those who look for their whole happiness in this poor earthly world. . . ."

In the Paris National Library there is preserved a manuscript of Pliny, once owned by Petrarch. On one page of this manuscript there is a drawing made by Petrarch's own hand; it represents the valley of Vaucluse, a cliff from which a spring flows, on the summit of the cliff a chapel, while below is shown a heron, with a fish in his beak; under the drawing is an inscription written by him in Latin: "My beyond-Alpine solitude."

His modest domain was situated in this valley, not many kilometers from Avignon.

Where, then, did Laura live in this now dull, old and dusty Avignon? It is assumed that it was near the present town-hall, in the street Doré. She was buried in the church of the Menorite brothers, in one of the chapels. But which? The church was destroyed during the Revolution, almost a century and a half ago. It is known, however, that it contained two chapels—the Holy Cross and St. Anne. Which of these sheltered her tomb? Again, it is assumed that it was the latter, as it was erected by her father-in-law, Signor de Sade. In the year 1533, King Francis I, in passing through Avignon, commanded that the half-demolished tomb, situated in the chapel, be opened; for he was assured by the citizens of Avignon that precisely here rested Laura's remains. Bones were found in the tomb. Whose? Were they really Laura's? It was impossible to decipher the name inscribed on the tomb.

COMRADE DOZORNY

The Story of N. N.

I WAS then twenty years old, I lived with my sister on her estate in the neighborhood of Orloff. I remember, as clearly as if it happened today, that I needed another shelf for my books. My sister suggested:

"Why don't you send for Kostin?"

Kostin came that same evening and took the order. We got into quite a conversation, and became so interested in each other that before long we might have been taken for friends.

He was my own age. In addition to his inherited

trade—his late father having also been a carpenter—
he had still another: having by his own efforts learned
to read and write, he fell into the position of assistant
instructor in the school erected near the church by my
brother-in-law, and he even moved into the school-
house, leaving his mother, older brother and sister in
their hut in the village, as he had already grown
ashamed of peasant life; while quite apart from this,
also because his older brother, a self-contained, prudent,
sensible man, considered him an unmitigated fool. And
really, there was something strange about him.

He was very tall and handsome, and he had a slight
stammer. Like most stammerers he had a girl's complexion and frequently blushed upon the slightest pre-
text. He was singularly timid and shy, he could not
look into anyone's eyes longer than an instant during
a conversation. It was at once to be seen that he lived
in some sort of world of his own, that he was secretly
consumed with an inordinate vanity, with a terrible sen-
sitiveness and an agonizing envy of practically everything in the world, from which emanated his other
astonishing trait: an insatiable, perfectly idiotic curiosity
and apishness.

To be with him and carry on a conversation with him
was, indeed, exhausting. He did not converse, but only
went on asking questions. His entire conversation con-
sisted of insistent detailed questionings and pryings:

What, how and why? With relish he repeated every answer and at once asked the next question. He would hold some object associated with his work, perhaps something which needed repairing or already finished and returned, and he would attentively examine it, feel it, stroke it with his large hands—and all the while go on tormenting you: he would ask you literally about everything which the conversation chanced to touch; he would repeat the answers with an astonished and gratified smile, and, apparently, he would never suffer even a momentary doubt as to whether or not he needed to know what he tried to discover. Incidentally, he piously believed positively everything he was told. I once jokingly told him that human beings in America walked on their hands, and even let their hair hang down: he showed a pleased astonishment, repeated what I said and believed it. In general, he had no comprehension of jokes, not the least.

From morning until night, every free moment he utilized in study, in tireless simulation. He studied and aped everything he saw or heard, by no means happily, if with sufficient accuracy. What that man couldn't do! He repaired watches and accordions, my bicycle and shop scales; he bound books and mended quail shooters' reeds, secretly learned to play upon a fife and wrote verse. . . . But I can scarcely remember all the things he could do.

It goes without saying, he neither drank nor smoked —at this point his apishness yielded to the femininity which distinguished his nature and, incidentally, created an unpleasant impression; he dressed with discreet smartness—thin boots, lounge coat, embroidered blouse, new cap—he even carried a handkerchief. And, invariably, he had with him an iron walking-stick.

The school stood next to the church lodge. During the big holidays the peasants who came to mass always smoked and carried on lively conversations in the lodge while waiting for the service to begin. Kostin usually appeared before the others and attentively listened to everything that was being said, although he himself did not join in the conversation but sat to one side, eyeing something intently—a rolling-pin, a flatiron, a notched axe—a scarcely noticeable smile of satisfaction on his lips at this exhibition of peasant garrulousness and stupidity.

I often visited him in the evenings: he was always at home and always diligently working at something. A small lamp on the table cast a dim light, while he, all hunched, sat beside it. His blouse was open at the neck, belted with a silken cord with fringes. His face was clean, rather lean but round, his eyes were a greenish white, his hair a bright yellow, oiled and brushed to part on the side, and falling in a tuft over the forehead. On seeing me, he would light up friendlily and, slightly stammering and avoiding my eyes, immediately launch into questions. Sometimes he would extract a copybook from a drawer in the table and hand it to me with the observation:

"Here are some new ones. R-read 'em and give us a criticism."

I opened the copybook and read:

> *"A frolicsome stream in the meadow doth flow,*
> *Until it doth lure the swimmer to death,*
> *Nameless—why no one can know,*
> *To tell his tale he doth lack breath. . . ."*

"So it's an acrostic again?"

"Yes, an acrostic. You see, the word 'aunt' comes out. Of course, I wanted another word, but . . ."

I well remember my last visit to him.

It was in the late autumn, fateful days for him and for me—we were just about to start for the city, to begin our term of army service. A week of holidays arrived, there still remained this week of freedom. One morning, just before dawn, I remember going to Mass, stopping first at the church lodge. The little lamp was still alight, the lodge was crowded to overflowing with gaily attired girls, women and peasants, and was as full of smoke as a corn-kiln; the peasants were raising a racket with their loud talk, while the women and the girls, now and then glancing in the direction of the bedstead by the stove, whispered and giggled and nudged one another; the butt of their mirth, as to be expected, was Kostin. He sat there, with lowered eyes, scrutinizing something or other; upon his head was a high lambskin cap, his boots were encased in new deep galoshes, he had on a new warm coat of black cloth, his face was flushed from humiliation, but the same faint smile hovered on his lips. . . .

I visited him the same evening at the school. The mud was terrible, the darkness impenetrable. A fine drizzle went on falling. I wended my way through the park like a blind man, acutely aware of nothing but the darkness, the autumnal warmth, the fragrant warm putrescence of wet trees, the smell of their bark and the tickling moist dust on my face. At last a tiny dim light radiated a whiteness ahead of me—it was the familiar little lamp on the table close to a window in the school—it was the one and only light visible in the whole village, which had long been plunged in a dead sleep. Kostin sat quietly at his work—with manifest pleasure he was gluing thin layers of veneer on to someone's checkerboard. A tiny woman, with curls falling over sloping forehead, the young wife of the churchlodge keeper—not at all bad-looking if it were not for her insignificant little nose with small rabbit-like nostrils—sat behind a desk near the wall and stupidly, with an odd gaiety, watched him at work out of shining coffee-brown eyes. I was feeling down in the mouth and, feigning nonchalance and lightheartedness, I spoke of what worried me—the approaching journey to the city. To my extreme astonishment, Kostin by no means shared my feelings. On the contrary, the prospective journey deeply interested him and was to him a source of much joy.

"Oh, no," he said, proceeding animatedly with his work and speaking almost without a stammer, "I think I'd have begged them to take me, if they didn't want me. I do hope they'll send me to Poland. It's only a couple of steps from P-paris!"

And suddenly, nodding his head in the direction of his silent and stupidly smiling female visitor, he added:

"This silly woman is also shedding tears for me. Tells me she's fallen in love with me. And, really, w-what interest can she have for me?"

"There he is, barking a lot of lies! As if you meant anything to me!"

He laughed indifferently.

A week later he and I drove to the station by night, to meet our train which was leaving at six. I took him along in my *tarantass*.* During the entire journey, in a leisurely manner, he went on plying me with questions on the score of military service in other countries, while the *tarantass* rocked in the darkness and fog, the in-

* Springless four-wheeled Russian vehicle.

visible horses floundered their way through puddles, stumbling into ruts filled with water and mud. As we were approaching the station we saw the first reluctant, somber light of dawn, and the first vague contours of stark trees in the station yard. . . . I remember, we had to wait long for the train. At last, in the dead-pale dawn mist, in the distance, there appeared the white, heavy, densely clouding smoke, out of which emerged a black engine, slowly gliding out of the darkling sea of autumnal fields. . . . And again, for some reason, I remember: next to the carriage in which we seated ourselves was a convict carriage with iron bars across the small square windows, and near one of the windows, with a manacled hand clutching one of the bars, stood a lean old man with a *pince-nez* on his humped nose, with red eye-lids; and strange indeed seemed the *pince-nez* in conjunction with the convict's cap, which sat on the prisoner's head like a gray pancake without a visor. . . .

The city was full of great multitudes of peasants who, with a loud and worried babble, walked in the middle of the street. Before the doors of the Rural Board offices, where the prospective soldiers were received, a dense throng gathered all day. Heavens, what a din! Wails, howls, keening, the cries of the accepted recruits, wildly and desperately pulling at their accordions— all that savage and terrifying clownishness with which

the Russian joyously invests his grief, fanning its flame
within him only the more. In the examination hall, from
the entering door itself, which opened and closed continuously, and through which an icy dampness blew,
and to the very table at which the examiners sat, whence
resounded the extraordinarily loud calls of the military
commander, there stretched the horrible queue of naked
bodies—short-legged, lean (but invariably pot-bellied),
chalk-white, with a brownish rash from the bites of
cockroaches, where every body showed a broad strip
impressed by the pants-belt. The military commander,
standing behind the table, in the presence of the com-
mittee, flung a quick glance at me and shouted something in a particularly loud voice. He was young, handsome, energetic, in a tight-fitting uniform; his short hair
was wavy, his curling moustaches projected, his bright
eyes lighted up the face with a vigilant flame. Kostin,
seated and pulling off his boots, his face flushed with
excitement, turned to me in an exultant whisper:

"And is that the chief himself?"

Within an hour he was passed for the army. And
within a fortnight he and I parted company—for a very
long time, indeed for a whole twenty years. The circumstances of our next meeting were these:

It was in the autumn of the year 1919. Our army
had only just evacuated K. For various reasons I tarried for a while, using every subterfuge in the guise of

a very poor peasant. The town was already filling with Bolshevik authorities and institutions, with Red troops and supply transports; and the Chekists, under the command of some sort of Comrade Dozorny, were already working without letting grass grow under their feet. One frosty, sunny day I happened to be walking along the main street. I walked past the cathedral, looked at the bare city park looming opposite; then I followed the pavement alongside former government offices, now adorned with red flags. A square faced these buildings, and a road led from this square downward toward the bridge by which one crossed the river. And lo, at the very instant that I reached the entrance of the former court-house, there appeared from the top of the hill a small cavalry detachment flying upon me at full speed, followed by a long and powerful gray car. It all happened so unexpectedly and the cavalcade paused so suddenly before the entrance that involuntarily I paused. At the same instant a tall man in a fur cap and an elegant officer's coat with a white lambskin collar and extremely smart officer's boots sprang from the car. His pale feline face with yellow moustaches was flushed with the excitement of his fast drive, his whitish eyes were dilated. He glanced in my direction and, running, rushed toward me.

"N-nikolai Nikolayevitch, is it y-you?" he gave a

slight gasp, as he flung the question at me, and flushed to his eyes.

And, without giving me time to answer, he added in a painful stammer:

"An' I, I'm Kostin—Dozorny . . . I've heard a l-lot a-a-bout you. . . . W-whew, w-what a l-lot—too much!"

And, turning to the two Bashkir soldiers sitting in the car with rifles in their hands, he shouted, as he ran into the entrance:

"To the park with him!"

Without being subjected to a search, I was marched at a fast pace across the square, and through the park —toward the rising slope hanging over the river bed. Then they shouted:

"Turn about face! Back to the river!"

I turned, as commanded. Then, instantly, I pulled a revolver from the pocket of my peasant belt and fired into the Bashkir snout at my left, and immediately fell backwards from the slope. The other snout fired at me; then, like the fool he was, ran back for help. I broke an arm, but all the same, got away.

ADVENTURE WITH A HANDBAG

THIS terrible adventure began simply, happily and smoothly.

It happened in the good old days, in the spring.

I was young, care-free, credulous. I was living in Moscow, and I was getting ready for my first journey to Constantinople, a circumstance which gave wing to my spirits, making it particularly easy for me to arrive at decisions, to guide my conduct, to have confidence in life.

At last the day for my departure grew very near, and as I began to pack for the journey I saw that my old handbag was by far too small and too dilapidated, and I immediately set out for the English Shop, on the Kuznetsky, to buy a new one, which would be larger and more solid.

What is a handbag? It is the closest, most intimate friend a human being has—at least, while he is traveling —and hence, it called for not a little intelligence and deliberation, for the shrewd judgment usually gained by experience, for the farsightedness which omits no future consideration, and, at the same time, in order to choose the thing practically, one had to make sure that it would not act as a detriment or violate one's aesthetic taste, the neglect of which was apt at times to make the most practical purchase loathsome. As for the handbag, with which this tale is concerned, I acquired it on a wholly different plan: without utilizing any of the rules of wisdom enumerated above, without thought or reflection, in the most casual haste, and, in any case, with rare success. This, I must confess, it had seemed to me at the beginning—and not without reason: the handbag, at the first glance, was irreproachable.

To this day I vividly remember the circumstances of the purchase. I entered the shop in high spirits, feeling thoroughly alive. I was in that pleasant frame of mind which is always evoked on entering a shop that is expensive, opulent, hence calm, spacious, well arranged, and the main thing is that you are long known there, and not only that but seemingly loved; where the attendants, resembling those at good hotels, meet you with a particular kind of smile, so that you immediately feel flattered and instantly become transformed into a fop and you make haste to dissemble in the rôle of precisely that kind of young society man who is held in restraint by this smile alone.

I remember how, responding to greetings, while I stuck my cane-head into the left-hand pocket of my great-coat so that its end was thrust out behind my shoulder, I strode rapidly down the carpets, through the various departments of the shop, and casually boasted that I was going away on a distant journey and that I would be away for quite a time; then, entering the traveling department, I nodded my head in the direction of the first handbag which happened to meet my eyes, a handbag of handsome brown-yellow leather, and, without as much as asking the price, merely asked to have it sent with the bill to my apartment in the "Rag Fair." I, of course, immediately comprehended that, in my foppery, I had over-reached the mark, and that the price of the handbag, when I came to discover it, would cause me to sigh. But this thought, this mood, instantly vanished in the realization that never before had I had such a superb thing, and that I could make up for the cost by practising economy on other traveling necessities. . . . It was quite a chance glance that made me cognizant of this handbag—and not in vain.

I repeat: quite unlike most purchases, which enchant you in the shops, while on closer and more deliberate inspection at home they bring complete disillusionment, my handbag, once in the "Rag Fair," proved worthy of my enthusiasm. When I first saw it in the shop it dazzled me with its locks, with the quality of its leather and with its superb workmanship, so that I, finding it necessary to make yet other purchases for my journey, hurried as fast as I could to return home, hurried as though to keep a love tryst. The handbag was already there, in the "Rag Fair"; as if awaiting my coming, it calmly reposed on the divan in the room, all done up in thick blue wrapping-paper and tied with a strong, slender rope. After my shopping, performed in haste, I literally ran into my room and rushed toward the divan. Quickly I cut the rope and tore the wrappings off—and, lo, my new friend and fellow-traveler appeared to me in all his glory: large, heavy, solid, well-disposed, with all the splendid gloss of new superb leather, with mirror-white locks, nobly aromatic, squeaking like satin. . . . You can easily imagine with what emotion I opened it, spread it out, saw for the first time its virginal wombs, its large pocket of dark-red morocco leather in the under-part of the upper half!

Thus it rejoiced me all the way to Odessa. All the while I delighted in the mood of my enrichment, in the thought of the quality of my possession. Picture me sitting at the table in the dining-car; I am bumped and tossed about, as I try, not without spilling, to pour out the red Bordeaux wine into a low thick glass tumbler; I gaze at the tables, at my neighbors, at the gay multicolored splendor ever present in dining-cars; then I drink my coffee and smoke a good cigar; while at the same time I have a mental vision of my coupé compartment with the already opened bed, the electric light under the rosy lampshade on the tiny bedside table—and *it*, my pride: it reposes in the stretched net above the bed, packed tight with traveling necessities, and it drowses and sways, together with all the travelers bound for Kieff and Odessa! Returning to my coupé, I quench my thirst with a pleasant drink; then I undress, extinguish the light, fall into a drowse—and again indulge in the same thought, the same emotion: night, the railway car, darkness, everything flies, tears along, jumps, and *it* is here, with me, in this net. . . . I even experienced a certain gratitude toward it!

Well . . . and then we arrived in Kieff, changed to another train, also a sleeper, an express, and when I awoke I was already in Odessa; all the passengers were washing, dressing or sipping tea or coffee, brought by the train attendants. . . . In Odessa we stopped at the "Petersburg." The handbag, of course, rested in the vestibule, while I took a cab to the steamship office, then lunched at the restaurant of the "Petersburg" on roast duck, drinking it down with a bottle of white Lachrima Christi, and, having settled the bill, and, once more in the company of the handbag, I set out for the Quarantine Harbor. . . .

The steamer was already preparing for departure. It turned out to be an old boat, which must have seen much; it was built low, with a heavy poop, with a deep setting—it all indicated, thought I, that it was a calm, steady ship. It had another pleasant aspect, it had almost no passengers; only at the last moment did two other first-class passengers arrive: some sort of Roman Catholic priest and a sickly woman, attired in mourning, from some embassy; so that my handbag and I had a whole cabin at our disposal. The handbag occupied the upper berth, while I took for myself the lower. Presently there became audible above us the stamp of sailors' feet, a din arose on deck, the sirens sounded, commands were shouted, the clicking of the telegraph apparatus was heard in the round-house, the pier began to recede from the steamer. . . .

At sunset we were already far out to sea, and I cannot remember a calmer, a steadier motion than that made the whole evening by our ship, and later in the soft dusk of a night at sea, with the soft wind blowing and increasing in strength. After I had had my fill of it in the poop, at ten o'clock I turned in and was already in my berth. I was beginning to plunge into a pleasant drowse, slowly rising and falling with the ship, tossing now to the right now to the left, suddenly at times conscious of the noisy impact of a wave as it struck the outer wall with the effect of a waterfall, and again evenly, quietly quivering from the gentle rhythmic tremors which came somewhere from the heart of a machine . . . when suddenly, just at the moment when I had wholly vanished somewhere, I was borne upward as on a swing, and then flung downward, and there was a deafening roar as of thunder, so that I savagely sprang from my berth, fully assured that the steamer had struck something and that in another instant the sea would surge into the cabin—and at once I received such a blow upon my legs that I lurched head downward under the bellowing wash-basin, but luckily, I did not succeed in reaching it, for the floor suddenly gave way under me and I again rolled toward my berth, once more overcome by some sort of thunder. . . . Then—there was a peal of merriment!

This much was clear: the ship rolled fearfully! But this thunder, this roar? This blow on my legs? What struck me like that? Terrible above all else was the instant of expectation of some new blow, while I was rolling about in my berth. At this instant, however, I became adroit; I fell into my berth with my chest downwards and, snatching across the partition at some press-button, I turned on the light. And what did I see? Amidst the din of the waves, the whistling of the wind, the creaking of the partitions, something alive was prancing about the floor of the frenziedly flying cabin! Yes, something alive, alive! But what? The handbag, of course! It was it that had deafened with thunder, that had come down flying from the upper berth to the floor with a crash, and later struck me across the legs. . . .

Now, at liberty, it ran about the cabin like one possessed. It was set on obtaining vengeance for the submission forced on it as it lay through the whole journey in nets and pretended to be my chattel, a soulless handbag. And it suddenly awakened to life and went on a devil's own rampage: smooth, slippery, heavy, like a paving-stone, packed by me to roundness, to bursting, in wild and frolicsome gaiety it now rushed upon me, upon my berth, and beat with its forehead against the foot of the berth; now, making a spring, turned somersaults as it flew under the wash-basin, and from there toward the door, and from the door toward under the bull's-eye. . . .

The wash-basin, tossing, like a drunkard, gasped for

breath, desperately caught at the air with its hole, gurgled and choked on a roar, the partitions creaked and squeaked, the bull's eye ever and again fell with its dark glass upon the onrushing waves which, coiling, beat upon it with a thick muddy spittle which ran in abominable arabesques and lace-like forms, while the handbag became more and more enraged and, without taking pity on itself, tore its wonderful hide and in a frenzy beat with its locks and corners against anything which came its way. . . .

It was necessary to make haste and to fling oneself on this mad fellow, to trample upon him down, to press him to the floor, to force him under the berth! But at this moment the floor again gave way under me, rearing up on end—and the handbag rapidly glided from under my body, gave me a good one on my pate and, whirling, rumbling, of its own accord made a dash for under the berth. Instantly I turned over, and was quite ready to push it in farther with a blow, but it suddenly sprang forward like a rubber ball, soaring, and made for the door. As it happened, I had turned in the same direction in which it was rushing—under the iron net of the berth, dreadfully grazing my shoulder. . . .

Should I go on with the description of this odious battle? There was neither an end nor bounds to it. I also lost my reason, I also was driven to fury. At the beginning I still thought that it was all merely the play of my imagination—that the handbag merely seemed to me alive, animated; at first I was frightened only in a self-interested way—I was afraid that it would go all to pieces, and I rushed, really, to help it, to make it possible for it to pause, to restrain itself. . . . But no! It was not merely a toy, not merely a source of diversion for the wind and the waves, not merely a senseless object involuntarily flying high and low, with the motion of the cabin! It was apparent that it was consciously happy in this Hades of the ship's rolling, which gave it such a marvelous chance to slip to the floor and let loose its diabolic frenzy, in order to incense me, to provoke me to fight, and unsparingly to strike wildly and aimlessly. If someone else could have only seen how agile it proved, how swift, how artful, how well-aimed and painful were its blows, how shrewd, strong and spiteful a creature it suddenly revealed itself to be! Nor, for that matter, was I the sort that gives in readily. I fought to the death, with my arms and legs—and at times rewarded the enemy with such cuffs that he, in desperation, would almost scramble up on to the wash-basin, which was turning its soul inside out from sea-sickness. I gnashed my teeth—oh, if only someone would come to my help! But who could help me? I thought of shouting—but that would be the supreme ignominy; in any case, who would hear me? Only the men of the sea-watch did not sleep. I gasped for breath, was wet with perspiration, tossed about my cabin in a shameless disheveled state, prayed to God for a dagger: oh, if I only had a dagger, and at once—with what rapture would I have thrust it into the side of this vile creature! But where was the dagger to come from? And what was a dagger to such an enemy!

It all ended in my flight. "Be thou accursed!" I shouted at the creature just before dawn. "Run about and carry on to your heart's delight!"—And, donning what garments I could, I fled from the cabin.

Up on deck there was the cold, ice, desolation, storm; ever and again, with foamy noisy tails the white waters strongly smelling of the sea swept the main deck. Avidly I drew into my chest the fresh air; I stood there, shaken, holding on to the lintel of the round-house. Already it was quieting down, and the first daylight appeared. The deck before me was dashing unto the cloudy heavens, which were growing lilac-tinted, and these same heavens seemed to disappear into some abyss; then suddenly the sea plateau opened, reared, rising to the perpendicular, and thus it bore down upon me, in green-gray hollow-indented mountains, which drove before them a dust of foam, resembling smoke. I left the round-house, to rush headlong into the wind, or, as the poets say, into the icy wings of the gale—and, with my cap shapelessly blown out, in a single zig-zag flew on to the poop, just at the moment when, with its broad rear, the poop was soaring upward; all the rest of it, all that clumsy bulk, which was immediately before me, under me—the deck, the round-house, the funnel, and the desperately wailing rigging—inclined prow-ward, bowing to the sea, and, with agonized joy, plunging into it up to the shoulder, up to the throat, and I suddenly saw how small and afflicted was our old black barge in this vast, savagely desolate circumference of water, drowning high the horizons, caught up in the tousled heavens. But what had this picture to do with me? I, seeing that the sea was nevertheless quieting down, that morning was approaching, set my teeth, and muttered malignantly, passionately (to the handbag, of course):

"Well, you just wait, just wait!"

And, really, what could I do to it?

A SIMPLE PEASANT

IT was Lubka's second winter at the home of the land-owners Panin, in Izvaly, when Ignat was hired on the estate as cowherd.

He was in his twenty-first year, she in her twentieth. He came from a poor family in Chesmenka, one of the villages composing Izvaly; she from a like one in Shatilovo, not many versts from Izvaly. It was said of her, though, that she was half "blue-blood," an illegitimate daughter of the Shatilovo proprietor. Furthermore, in all the duties of her daily work, Lubka, as house maid, rubbed shoulders with the gentlefolk. Because of this, the more the young herdsman burned for the beauty of the girl, the shyer he became. And the shyer he became, the more he thought of her, the more sullen and silent he grew.

Lubka's eyes were black and bright, frank and almost criminally clear. From her mistress, a graying widow who smoked thin, scented cigarettes, she stole, deftly and quietly, both soap and perfume. At times lively and naïve, she looked younger than her twenty years, at other times older, a woman who had tasted everything. Before she was fourteen she was raped by the old rake Zybin, the district commissioner of Shatilovo; and now she permitted a lot to the two young masters of the Panin place without any fear of losing her head. But to Ignat, who as yet did not know women, the relations between men and women were becoming more frightening and desirable. In all of Izvaly, indeed, there was not a more complex, secretive fellow than this Ignat. Even riding in his work cart directly to the grain sheds to get straw for the animals, he would never answer openly to the simple question, "Where are you going?" And, avoiding Lubka's glances, without raising his sullen eyes, ashamed of his ragged open-fiber, cloth-wrapped shoes, his worn cap and tattered coat, he would watch her from beneath his eyebrows. And her calm shamelessness, which he dimly understood, awed and fascinated him.

The behavior of the two young masters of the estate also increased Ignat's love. . . . The two of them—Alexis Kuzmich, an officer who had already spent some time in the Caucasus for a certain delicate, private treatment, a man the same age as Ignat, and Nikolai, the younger, the same age as Lubka, a lad who had shifted frequently from one institution of learning to another—came home during the winter season only on the great holidays. This year the younger squire had come home first, to celebrate *Maslenitsa*. Lubka was unusually animated and went about with a particularly frank and open air, without, however, being frank with anyone. Her self-possessed eyes sparkled, and heightened spots appeared in her swarthy cheeks. Dark-haired, strong, working her elbows, swishing her white starched apron, she rushed about in a green woolen dress, from one thing to another, from the servants' quarters to the house and from the house to the servants' quarters, over the trodden path through the snow-filled yard. During the Shrovetide, when the holiday smoke rose from the chimneys above the firs and pines in the garden, standing gloomy and dull in the gray days, Ignat could not avoid witnessing more than once the play of the young masters with the girl.

Once, at dusk she flew out of the house with an angry, flushed face, her hair streaming behind her. Nikolai Kuzmich, laughing and shouting something, ran out onto the steps after her. And there he stood on the thawing stoop, a stoutish fellow, big-headed, with a dull and authoritative profile, in his white silk blouse and patent-leather boots.

That night, later, Lubka, gay again and panting, bumped into Ignat in the dark hall of the servants' quarters.

She stopped for an instant, before racing on.

"He tore my petticoat and he gave me a whole bottle of Persian Wisteria," she said, unexpectedly. "Here, smell that!"

And in a second she was gone.

The herdsman stood, rooted to the spot, dully staring into the darkness, a darkness heavy with the smells of the kitchen, of dog-smell from the animals whose eyes glittered like twin garnets as they passed in and out of the hallway; but he was alive only to the overpowering sweet fragrance of the perfume and the still more overpowering odor of hair, of carnation pomade, and the woolen dress with perspiration under the arms. . . .

Then Alexis Kuzmich, the officer, came home—lean, with sharp, brown eyes, a long, pale grayish face flecked with powdered red pimples. Her hair freshly waved, her body pinched into a tight-fitting corset, Lubka's mistress came heavily out upon the steps by the drive, her flesh shaking as she walked. And as the bells of the *troika* tinkled gaily from the hill-road, she waved her handkerchief, continually, until the driver reined in at the door. The young officer, bawling something in a loud and imperious tone, and apparently not deigning to notice whether anyone listened or not, threw aside the fur laprobe with a flourish one sees in front of some fashionable restaurant, and ran up the steps, lithe and easy in his movements, his legs very thin and somewhat bowed in his small, shiny boots, his silver spurs clinking. With a jerk of his shoulders, he adjusted the wide Nokolayevsky military coat with its high beaver collar.

It was Ash Wednesday Eve. The holiday had come late this winter, and at times the weather gave a hint that spring was pushing northward. From early morning the sun shone, the blue skies reflecting from the snow, and the long icicles around the house dripping into puddles on the ground. But early in the afternoon, the day turned sullen, raw and penetrating. The garden near the house darkened and turned chill, brooding in the early shadows. Unmindful of the rawness and the wind, Lubka kept on dragging in packages from the officer's sled. The cowherd watched her, watched the way her body moved.

He stood on the wide, dirty landing before the peasants' quarters, the place odorous of pan-cake smoke.

Large flakes of snow were falling, instantly thawing. In front of the threshold of the house, before the steps, a number of newly arrived rooks walked through a puddle, strutting with importance. A peasant and the woman cook, her skirt tucked inside her belt, showing a man's high boots, carried out of the quarters a huge tub, a stick through its handles. Thick yellow mash steamed in the tub. The wolf-hounds appeared suddenly, in a pack, shaking and hunched together, their tails hanging between their legs, and began devouring the feed. The cook's boy, in a red, holiday shirt, stirred the mash with a spade, occasionally lifting it out of the tub to strike at the crowding dogs as they pushed and growled. The yard was already showing bare spots where the earth here and there was darkening through the snow.

The dogs withdrew from the tub, finished, their snouts covered with the yellow mash, and rolled and rubbed themselves on the ground, and then streaked out through the yard toward the garden behind the house. Side by side with the beautiful Strelka, the black-eyed Borzoi with the silky white fur, ran a large red house dog, ferociously showing its teeth, growling and choking, and preventing the other wolf-hounds from coming near her. Ignat, impelled by desires, followed after the dogs. But in the alley they all turned off, bounding over the path under the gnarled old apple trees until they disappeared. Ignat went on, through the house garden and into the wide fields. The snow was driving down obliquely. He removed his cap, and from its torn cotton lining he dug out a cherished 20-kopeck piece.

Along the garden wall he went, through many back fields, and on toward the village which showed its darkly thawed-out hut-roofs on the hill. The snow along the way lay in mounds, yellowish, rutted with sled runners, the droppings of horses pounded in the tracks running green with water in the tramped ground between the huts and out-buildings. At the window of a particularly bleak and unhealthy-looking hovel, under whose walls a few chickens dozed with their heads under their wings, Ignat knocked. A yellowish old face flattened itself against the inside of the pane. Ignat held up the 20-kopeck piece. The old woman pulled on a pair of heavy, ragged felt boots, covered her head with a short pelt and led Ignat across the road into a shed with a strong iron door. She shoved a bottle into the deep pants pocket which he held open.

Behind the sheds on the slope of the wind-blown hill, he stood in the snow, thinking of Lubka. Then, throwing his head back, he drank the contents of the bottle to the final drop, without a breath. He hid the empty bottle in the snow, feeling the poison course hot and pleasant through his entire body. He squatted in the snow, awaiting the effect to come. In a moment or two he relaxed, falling back upon the ground, laughing in the joy of his drunkenness, and crawled up the hill into a deserted meadow.

When, later, he came to his senses, he stared about him for a long time, straining to realize where he was. He felt himself weightless and small. He was frozen through. A raw wind blew. It was getting dark and the snow had stopped. With sudden fear, he remembered that he had not yet brought in the straw to start the morning fires, for it was one of his chores to bring piles of it every evening to the back of the house, placing it in readiness in the space beneath the steps. He sprang up and ran through the village, and through the garden near the house. His head was heavy, but his body light, all his senses strangely sharpened, sharpened more by the wind against his face. It was a sweet wind; one felt like swallowing it with a full chest. He remembered now, too, that he had forgotten a rope on the back steps, and panting and splashing his heavy shoes along the wet snow, he veered from the path to the house. In the half light, under the steps, stood a man, squeezing some-one to the wall. Hearing Ignat's steps, he turned upon him.

"What do you want?" he demanded.

It was Alexis Kuzmich—his voice, his long pale face, his long narrow head, close-cropped in the military style. Lubka, pressed against the wall, held the officer

by two fingers, and did not release his hand. The herdsman backed off, his eyes riveted to her apron. He stood
for a moment in the yard, then slouched away, again
feeling a pain in his stomach and a weakness in his shoulders and his legs. Rain clouds hung over the garden in
sullen dark whorls. The rising western wind rippled
the black puddles, and there was in the air a soft, in-
toxicating moistness, the growing strength of an early
spring challenging the winter.

The following day winter conquered, snow fell
thickly, and toward evening the fields were lost behind the curtains of the storm. Lubka's lady drove out
to call upon a neighboring estate. Alexis, his military
spurs clanking, stepped out on the back steps and
shouted across the yard to hitch up Korolek. Bending
over the dogs, which hung about the stoop, snow on
their backs and heads, the officer petted and played
with one after another, scratching behind their ears,
and shaking them passionately, teasing and muttering
nonsense to them through his bared teeth.

Lubka, carrying a dish of fish to the servant quarters,
passed by him. He gave her a side glance, and lunged
among the dogs. "Ah, you pups, you devils, you," he
shouted.

It was the last day before Lent. Over the hill, from
as far off as the river, came the sound of voices, songs,
drunken shouts, the tinkle of sleigh bells and the ring-

ing and the booming of the larger bell of the village. The village shop-keeper, the shoemaker, the policeman, the peasants, all were sledding with their guests, their ladies, maids and relatives. It was gay and sad. One could feel both the peak and the finish of the holiday. When the horse, Korolek, was hitched, the officer, in a smart gray little coat with fur cap, went into the house and came out again, pulling the laughing Lubka, who was beaming now and rouged. She wore a fur coat with a cheap brown collar and a green dress pinned up above her boots. Her head was bound around with a gray shawl and, bobbing with laughter and good spirits, she stomped down the steps. Ignat, having brought up Korolek, held the ginger-colored colt by the bit, as the young animal pawed the driveway, flashing a wicked eye sideways at the officer's bright silk scarf which showed from under his collar. His neck was thin and covered with half-healed pimples and scars. Ignat's eyes were dropped to the level of Lubka's white skirt, to her rough half-boots oiled with lard. . . . As he dragged off later in his work sled toward the barns, he held hard the lead-rope in his hands, and with it belabored the lean, bony back of his nag. Korolek, snorting his vitality, the fresh snow driving in his face and into his hot nostrils, little bullets of hard snow flying from his hoofs and clicking against the dashboard, sailed on by, covering the herdsman and his nag with the dancing veil of his breath, and grew smaller and smaller in the distant blurr descending whitely on the fields. The snow fell in huge flakes upon the sleek back of the well-fed Korolek, and on the fur cap, the shoulder-straps, the shiny small boots with the silver spurs braced against the sled's iron footrail. In his left hand, in a suède glove, the officer held the pale blue reins. With the other he suddenly reached for the head in the gray shawl and pressed his fur cap against it. . . .

And Ignat decided, definitely, to swap his accordion, his sole treasure, with Yashka, the workman, for a pair of old boots. When he had finished hauling the straw and firewood, he did not go into the village streets to join the throng which crowded together in a dark cluster under the roof of the last hut near the church. There, accordions vied with one another, gaily and madly, all of them drowned in turn by the wind and the songs. The peasant square was ringed with smoke and whirling girls were dancing through the air like witches. But Ignat, sinking heavily in the snow and slush, pulled himself past the square toward the brightly lighted house of the village shop-keeper, and stood there for two hours, his eyes glued on the snow-rimmed window in whose bright golden square the passing shadows showed the movements of the dancers.

II

Lent was gray and monotonous.

A cruel wind blew day after day, the fields stood white and pale, the dark firs and pines sang their sad song in the blue-shadowed garden, and the rooks, which had arrived too early, went into hiding. The officer, Alexis Kuzmich, had long since ended his visit home and departed. But Nikolai Kuzmich tarried on. Once Ignat drove his work sled up to the back steps of the house. The sled scraped the side of the steps, bumping open the storm-door hanging ajar, and the young master, who was under the steps with Lubka, rose from the piled straw, laughing. Lubka, fixing her hair, looked out serenely.

"It's all play to you," she said. "But the whole village will soon be barking. Ignat," she stared at the young herdsman, "why don't you make a wife out of me?"

Ignat blushed and frowned. He made not the slightest retort to her words, but from that day on jealousy and envy began to grow within him. Chewing his black bread, he jogged his cart along the road to the granary, giving the manor house a sidewise glance because he knew only too well what was going on within it. The dogs tore after him, a bouncing brown pack. From the old manure heaps came the squeak and scurry of mice, and the dogs, rooting in the straw, smelling and sniffing, quivering and whining, would suddenly pounce on their prey, rapacious and precise. At the granary, Ignat would coax in the soft sleek Strelka, the dog with the eyes so limpid and feminine. Once inside, he would shut tight the creaking doors. The air was thin with the cold smell of earth and the faintly warm scent of golden wheat stalks. Across the half darkness of the immense triangle above him, along the eaves, the beams and crossbeams of which were covered with a thick gray layer of velvet dust from the last summer's threshing, a cold pale light cut through the long crack of the doors. The wind swished against them, and swept along the threshing floor. . . .

On a clear, sunny day of his third week at home Nikolai Kuzmich departed. Spring had come on suddenly. The straw-thatched roofs of the barns and the outhouses thawed in a day and the old gray thatch shone like gold in the sun, contrasting brightly with the high blue sky which softened the soul. The young colts and cows, still fuzzy with their winter coats, napped and basked in the sunshine. The damp, thawing snow glistened sharp and silvery. A *troika* stood by the guest entrance in the shade, beside a blue puddle. The puddle reflected both the sky and Lubka's white apron. Out of the house came Nikolai Kuzmich, his fur coat thrown over his short jacket. With him walked his mother, the lady of the manor. They said good-bye many times over, and from the sled the young man turned back to shout farewells. The runners slushed through the trembling little rivulets of melting snow, dotted with the manure accumulations of winter, now like wet tobacco. Wherever water shone in the ruts, the thin-legged horses, with their tails smartly tied in knots, flashed the steel of their shoes with showy smartness. It was warm in the sun. Chattering rooks perched in the branches of the firs near the house, the trees now flaring freshly green. But in the shade one still felt a little of the keen north wind. Lubka, on the steps, stood chilled, her cheeks tinged bluish. . . . The sled disappeared beyond the hill. She hummed, thoughtfully, *"Just a couple in a troika."* . . . Then pulled herself together, and turned into the house. A little later·and she was outside on the steps in back. Ignat, who was at work in the yard, came over to her. Dully, without moving, she looked at him. He came up close and suddenly took her by the wrists. At once they were both confused. Half in play, pulling and tugging, their hands tangled together, neither knew what to say. Suddenly Lubka frowned.

"Here," she said. "Let go! . . . What nerve!"

And pulling away from him, she went inside and slammed the door.

Alone, outside, the yard seemed despairingly chill and bare, its winter-bitten trees and bushes lost in the lonely shadows of the dusk. The open path seemed wide and inviting. And once more Ignat, glowering and mean, trudged along the pathway to the village, to the old woman who sold the vodka. And once more he woke up in the dusk, in the meadow, frozen to the bone, amazed. Over him stood a sentineled tree, brooding at his guilt, drooping long moustachios of hoar frost, a silhouette against the lowering sun. Beyond the hill, the sky loomed vast without limit.

"I'm no match for her," he said, grimly getting to his feet. "I'm done for."

From that evening on he never looked at the house when he jogged by toward the barns and sheds. He never answered Lubka when she spoke to him. Lent ended, and so the Holy Week, too. No more snow remained except in the shaded gulleys and a light lemon down appeared on the willows near the villages; around the villages the blue-black plow lands stretched immense, the sun beat warm, glassy rays trembled on the horizon, larks sang high in the air, and the green-damp paths, the furrows and the roads were drying out. Fresh smelling grass pushed through the earth. Ignat had long since begun driving his herds to the pastures through the Miliutin woods, which still stood winter-stripped and barren, but providing, under foot, a bed of dried oak leaves, sprinkled with snowdrops. The cows mooned lazily in the clearing where the sun shone warmest.

There was nothing for them to eat; they lay on the ground, patiently, and the rooks settled on their very backs, brazenly picking loose hair for their nests. Ignat wove a new whip, idly gazing into the sunny distance, and seeing the roads already covered with the dust which pleasantly suggested summer. His stolid young features were tanning in the dry, windless April days.

He was happy when he had money. Choosing a dry spot in the field, he spread out his torn, tattered coat, placed the bottle on it, pulled the soggy bread from his pocket, and the cold boiled potatoes. Soon his head began to swim blissfully. The sunny southern horizon beyond the graying steppes quivered, a thin stream rising blue above the baked manure heaps strewn over the fields. The cows swam pleasantly in the haze. Strange . . . he was still expecting something! Drunk, he still felt it; he felt his life had become tied up with Lubka's life—to his own undoing. Something must be done—to conquer her, to become her equal, to call out her love. Otherwise, even though he had his will of her, she would not love a simple peasant. . . . And the spring clamored for love. Trembling, first on the foreknees, then awkwardly raising their backs, one cow after another got to its feet. . . . The giant bull, his broad forehead shaggy with hair, came lumbering toward them, shaking glassy threads of spittle at his jowls, and, suddenly, swelling with power, reared on his hind legs.

Ignat's heart stopped within him. He fell backward against the dry black earth. His eyes were closed, tears rolling from under his eye-lashes. He did not wipe them off, and flies buzzed and settled on them. He fell asleep and lay there until the sun, straight above him, baked his head and shoulders and awakened him. Afterward, he drove the herd back to the barns, ate in the peasant quarters without words, and went off to sleep in the carriage shed, where, against the stone wall, stood a high bedstead, knocked together with old boards and covered with straw and the rags of a red cotton quilt. After his night's sleep, he rose mean and sullen and drove out the herd, beating the cows so hard with his long cracking whip that welts formed on their backs.

He made up his mind to behave in such a way that would make the overseer beat him and discharge him from the estate. The coming summer, the inevitable return of the two young masters of the place—all of it frightened him; some time he might lose his head and from the corner of the house crack open the skull of Lubka or Nikolai with a brick! But, as it happened, one day, in May, when the woods were already flourishing a rich green growth, and flowers were twinkling from the grass, when even in the early morning it turned summer-like in the open meadows, and lilies-of-the-valley were emerging in the fresh dewy shadows, he saw a woman sitting in the clearing as he reached the pasture grounds. It was the pauper, the half-wit Thiona. Her burlap bag and stick beside her, she sat, all in tatters, her mouth agape, the lower part of her skirt wet, her eyes glistening in her puffed face. She was slightly drunk. When Ignat came up, she fell over backward with a repressed passionate giggle, baring her knees, and began to rub her big wrapped shoes along the grass. The burlap sack beside her contained both cake and vodka. And when he drank, Ignat let himself go. . . .

From then on, the half-wit began coming to the field almost daily. Waking at nights, he strained at times to cry: it was insulting, it pained him to think that he lived with a half-wit! He drove out his herd before the sunrise, in the cold, heavy dew. . . . At noon he drank. Now they both drank on his money. He drew his pay a month in advance. But even that came at last to an end. Thiona became angry, impudent, exacting; she no longer feigned being a half-wit. When Ignat came without vodka, she denied him, starved him, a week on end. Once she even cracked him over the head with her stick, ably and hard. He rose and slouched away, strangely and awkwardly weeping. His tears ended, he sat on a path and dully thought of the same old thing, of which he now thought continuously: where to get money? But there was no place to get it, no place to steal it. Already he'd drunk away his boots.

All the peasants on the place knew his story, and often they jibed at him at meal times. He turned deep red and kept silent. Suppose, now, Lubka heard of this. . . . But, lucky for him, the young masters did not come back. It was rumored that Nikolai Kuzmich was visiting a friend near Kharkoff, that the officer, Alexis, was engaged in maneuvers near Smolensk. And the lady of the manor herself was off for six weeks to Lipetsk and took Lubka with her. The place lapsed quiet and boring. The half-wit's visits became rarer and rarer—she chased from one village fair to another. The summer was nearing its end, hot and long. The river shallowed out, the cattle crunched through all the forage left, the black soil showed through the close-clipped stalks. The grain was ready, the wheat dried and fell to the ground. They began taking in the harvest. It was the end of July.

At the end of July, returning at sunset with his herd to the village, Ignat met the half-wit. She stopped and pointed to the woods.

"When I'm done, I'll come," he said, without raising his eyes.

But, to go without vodka? He stood sadly at the gates of the estate, looking toward the falling sun. Along the road, cutting slantwise over the hill, the peasants and their women, on dusty carts, were rattling home from the fields, the scythes, flails and rakes stuck out from the slats of the carts. The sun, the color of a raspberry, set, a vast and rayless globe, upon the dry purple haze beyond the river, beyond the fields already covered with links of sheaves. Ignat pushed through the gates, cut through the field, then past the garden toward the grain sheds. Ahead of him a dirty, curly-headed little girl kicked her small feet through the dust. Straining with its weight, she carried in her right hand a pail filled with freshly bought tar. Ignat quickened his pace to catch up with her, he glanced back, and then grabbed her tiny left hand in which she was tinkling some small coins. Her eyes went round with terror, her face twisted, and she screamed and tightened her fist, resisting like a little cornered beast. Ignat seized her by the throat and threw her on the ground. The child choked for breath and opened her fingers. He raked the money from her palm. Thirty kopecks.

Having bought the vodka, he went straight toward the woods. To the right was the cut harvest, the sheaves standing faintly light in the dusk. From his left a warm wind blew off the black plowed land, from the steppes. Ahead of him, above the dark fringe of the woods, Mars, red and huge, was rising. The cowherd stopped, suddenly, on the road. He recalled that it was today the lady of the estate was expected home, that a *troika* had been sent along the highroad for her and a peasant cart sent also to the station for her luggage. And soon, indeed, holding his breath to catch the sound, he heard the distant music of the harness bells.

All during the summer it had seemed to him that he might somehow escape the inevitable something which was to be. But now, he knew it really could not be done, he could not escape. It was coming nearer, looming larger as it came. . . . He stood for a time in the road, then went on.

At the crossroads he was deafened by the bells, the clattering of the horses, and the dust in the wake of the *troika* flew in clouds about his face. From farther down the road came the familiar rumble of the peasant cart. It was getting nearer. And a minute later Ignat saw on the dull starry sky the silhouetted yoke above the horse, the horse itself, and behind it Lubka, sitting in the cart. She flipped the reins over the horse's back and bumped up and down, rushing straight down upon him.

"Climb in! I'll give you a lift on home!" she sang out gaily, recognizing Ignat in the dusk.

He turned and caught up with the heavily loaded cart and hopped up, sidewise, to sit along the sideboards.

What Lubka talked about, he did not remember. He remembered only the first words, which struck him to the heart. Lightly, her deep voice like a song to him, drowning the rumbling of the cart, she cried:

"Well! Have you missed me much?"

He remembered only that moment when he suddenly seized the reins, and, pulling in the horses, he threw his legs inside the cart.

"Wait!" whispered Lubka, as simply as if they had lived together for many years. And this simplicity made his head swim. "Wait! You'll ruin my skirt, honey. Let me fix it. . . ."

III

Four years went by. It was December. Ignat, having served the four-year military period required of those who reach twenty-one, was returning from the city of Vasilkoff to his home village.

He had lived only three months with his wife. Soon after that July night when his fate had taken such a sudden turn, Lubka felt that she was pregnant; and the evil thought never left him that this had been the only reason she had married him. She told him she loved him, she found a job for his father, a sick old man, getting him work as herdsman on the estate; Ignat she clothed and equipped for his journey to his regiment, and at the station she saw him off with tears. . . . He beat her badly while he amused himself by showing off his new uniform to the whole village before he left, and, beating her, avenged himself for the young masters before him. She even dropped the child, miscarriage from the beating, but accepted it all as well-deserved. When they took him away to Vasilkoff with the recruits, she often enclosed money in her letters to him, and wrote him sweetly. But he did not believe a single word, lived in anxiety, in sadness, in continuous suffering, in jealousy, inventing the most truculent punishments for her imagined unfaithfulness.

On his furlough home two years before the end of his service, he had planned, all the way back, to kill her, if he should learn anything bad. On his arrival in the village he had made many inquiries. He learned that Lubka refused only the lazy ones. But she met him with such joy, denied all rumors with such simplicity and frankness, that his tensed arm fell to his side. In order to quiet him entirely, she said she was leaving her work on the Panin estate, and was going to move to their hut by herself, where she would wait patiently for his return, working in the meantime on a sewing machine and feeding herself that way. And he left for his regiment again, downcast, puzzled. Downcast and silent he remained for all his service, but efficient, accurate and thrifty, saving his pay, and any little bribes from fellow soldiers. He still had the hope of becoming the equal of Lubka, of becoming worthy of her real and unfeigned love. But suddenly her letters ceased. He wrote almost every week. No answer. He threatened, begged. She was silent. He began again to drink, and became dull and tired.

Nevertheless, his soldiering finished, he went back to Izvaly.

He had changed very much. He was thin now, tall and quite handsome. His leaden eyes were larger, his face seemed grayer and leaner. He shaved often. His reddish moustache was cut like a brush, his hair trimmed in the military "porcupine" style, and the skin of his scalp was visible through his short wiry hair. From Kieff to Orel he sat motionless in the train near his rough wooden trunk, which was painted walnut color, his boots and tea-kettle tied to the straps. He removed neither his cap nor the rough military coat which chafed his neck, gazed constantly at the floor and crunched on sunflower seeds. From Orel on he began to worry, and went to the refreshment stand at every station. In the railroad station of his native village, he ran into a former service comrade, had drinks, and left his trunk with the guard. The two quit the station and hired an old coachman who drove them, with the utmost speed of which his three-legged mare was capable, into the heart of the town. The two were excited and smoked one cigarette after another. They drove into the notorious district, where Ignat stayed for almost twenty-four hours with a small, short-legged, middle-aged brunette, who smoked with even more fervor than he. He came to himself in a field near the district, and with difficulty recalled that he had been severely beaten before they had kicked him out. It was a soft, white day; it snowed and the flakes stuck in the folds of his coat. He got up, shaky, feeling as sick as if he had been poisoned. . . .

To the village of Izvaly he was forced to ride in a freight car, together with a consignment of hogs which were so fat they sank on their tails, unable to stand. The hogs were destined for a wealthy landowner as breeding stock, and they were accompanied by the landowner's ancient gardener, a neat and quiet man, a former household servant. Besides the gardener, Ignat and the hogs, there was another passenger, a Jew, gray, curly-haired, large-headed and bearded, wearing glasses and a stovepipe hat and a long coat trailing to his ankles, navy blue in some places and sky blue in others, a coat with low-cut pockets. He was silent all the way, looked thoughtfully concerned, hummed some melody, and drank tea. The gardener napped. The hogs swayed on their haunches behind the wooden partition, over them a gray cloth blanket with crown and crest. It was getting dark, the wind and snow blew into the open door and whirred the damp straw off the floor. Flat white fields swept by, a slowly settling band of engine smoke riding with them, level with the train, like a hedge.

A heavy feeling of anxiety pressed on Ignat. He tied and retied his orange-trimmed neckpiece, his brow darkened, his teeth ground as his jaws moved up and down.

He stood by the door, chewing sunflower seeds and looking sidewise at the Jew. The Jew sat on a box turned upside down, holding a glass of tea in a large hand swollen with veins. The seed shells blew in the wind and some fell into the tea. The Jew looked up at Ignat through his spectacles. Ignat waited for the Jew to say something so that he could drive a boot into his stomach. But the Jew said nothing; only arose and poured the tea out, purposely near Ignat's feet in their flat and spacious military boots.

At the station where he got out in the darkness, Ignat found no fellow-travelers bound for his village. He was forced to sit and wait for the chance of someone to turn up. His hands were ice-cold, his head swam. It was half-past ten when the outline of the station had risen in front of him, with its familiar walls and lighted windows. The passenger train had just pulled out. In the third-class waiting room, cold and badly lit, heavy with smoke and body odors, one was forced to use one's elbows to get through, so many peasants were crowded in. Every minute the door squeaked open, slammed, and a fresh frosty gust of air rushed through the sullen waiting room, lifting the whirls of steam above the samovar in the main room. From the brighter illuminated ticket office and telegraph room there came without cessation the dribbling sound of a bell, as if someone had wound up an alarm clock and forgotten to turn it off. And in this crowded, ringing room, Ignat's temples throbbed.

He made inquiries here and there for fellow-travelers, walked about dully like a lunatic, but saw and noticed everything with an unusual clearness. The throng of coats and peasant pelts was thinning out. He went out on the station steps, allowing the others to pass him, stepping sideways before those ahead of him, staring at horses and sleds and at the cloud-flecked, moonlit skies. He smoked a cigarette, deeply breathing in the sweet winter air, together with the smoke, and returned, finally, to get his trunk. The refreshment counter man had already stripped his counter bare, piece by piece he had removed the oranges, cigarettes, the plates of sausage and the lone piece of sweaty cheese. The station master was leading by the arm a large elderly lady in a fur coat who was leaning on a crutch. Through the open door was visible the moonlit night outside, and the trees covered with white. The horses standing by the steps shook and grumbled. The noises of departing sleds died out, the hard snow crunching under the runners far on up the road. . . . Only a woman remained in the waiting room; she wore a new reddish fur coat and sat on a long wooden bench by the wall near Ignat's trunk. Ignat went over toward the bench, squatted down, pulled the little trunk up onto his back, and, suddenly recalling a distant spring when he was living with

Thiona, the half-wit, and was free of worries and free to drink good vodka and finish off with cold boiled potatoes, he strode out of the station.

He walked rapidly, determinedly, his boots squeaking in the snow. The fields were dead and empty. The moon was hiding behind the light clouds, the road stretching in the dark in front of him. . . . In Izvaly, he came back from his slow, dulled thoughts. Around him he saw the widely spaced-out houses of the village, all asleep. There was not one late light in the huts buried in the shadows and the snow. The air seemed quieter, the freshness sweeter. A restive rooster crowed somewhere in the yards.

He stood in front of his own empty hovel on the outskirts of the village near the gulley, not knowing what to do. A small hut it was, half-buried by the drifts. There was a lock on the door and one window boarded up. The snow at the open gates of the yard showed tracks of peasant shoes. A snow bank at the side of the house rose level with the roof. Ignat followed the path inside and sauntered around the yard. In an open shed in back someone's calf was sleepily trying to make itself comfortable for the night. . . .

A little way on, in Marey's hut, a dim light was burning. The glimmer came through a tiny window almost level with the high snow of the road. He went across and peered in at the pane. A spinning-wheel occupied almost all the tiny hut. A youngish woman with a firm, ruddy face, was spinning linen thread and making the room grumble with the noise of the wheel. Ignat knocked. She looked up with fear and surprise. He walked inside and set the trunk down. The girl, a mute from childhood, went over to the stove and began tugging at a shoestring dangling from a rough peasant shoe which hung from the bed above. Heavy with the first hours of sleep, the man above responded only with a husky coughing and grumbling as she pulled at the shoe. Finally, the old fellow, her father, began crawling down backwards, groping with the heavy wrapped shoe for his footing. Once down, he hobbled along the wall, leaning against it, trying to avoid stepping on one foot, which was apparently injured. He reached the bench near the table. Bearded, dishevelled, with bulging, blood-shot eyes, he looked half mad. Ignat pushed the trunk against the wall, and sat down at the table. The young woman, her hands clasped before her, stood staring by the stove.

Marey, having first asked a smoke, inhaled deeply, and let the smoke out slowly, gratefully, until his head and beard were lost in a cloud.

"Your missus?" he repeated. "Sure I've seen her. I see her walking from the church. . . . Didn't take much to living by herself there. Rather stay at the big house. The masters' place. Nobody much there though, either. They're both gone a long time now . . . to Moscow. They say she's gone and fired the overseer. Runs the whole show herself now. The big boss. Nothing small about her—your missus. She aims to please herself. . . . That's what. . . ."

"Yes, I know. I know," said Ignat. Preoccupied, he slid his fingernail back and forth along a dirt-filled crack in the table.

"Sure you know. . . . Well, you scare the hell out of her. She'll stop. Scare her. I got mine there engaged." He looked toward the dumb girl, still standing in the corner. "A person can't ever be sure, at that. He's a widower. And suppose he slips out of it? The hell! He needs a wife like her. Of course, she don't talk clear, but for work, she's first-class. I won't knock her. . . . Here, you now, you picked out a good one. And now where are you? Bad match, I'd say. Cut a tree your own size, as they say. . . ."

"I'll leave my trunk here with you for a while," said Ignat, without raising his eyes.

"Sure, leave it. Why don't you leave it?" Marey agreed.

He got up to the door to let Ignat out. The night was still frosty and clear. The skies were clearing of clouds, the moon, bright and full, rolled out in space, a slanting white streak of cloud moved rapidly toward the northern horizon. The shadows were deeper, the road sparkled.

"Winter, all right," grumbled Marey, withdrawing his head from the doorway, his nostrils tingling with the icy air.

Again Ignat went determinedly on, without once turning his neck in his rough army muffler to look back. He walked a little more than two versts, passed the other sleeping houses of the villages, and then set out toward the meadow along the hill-road. On the hill, he could see the familiar buildings of the Panin place, the dark clumps of trees in the front yard of the house, and the four lighted windows. He went toward the lower fields, at the foot of the hill, entered the gates, and crossed along the dam of the pond now covered with snow. Ahead of him were the rambling, gloomy sheds of the barn yard, looming darkly under the tall old trees. The sky seemed endless. The moon rolled to his right. Here and there shone large stars. A rabbit sat upright on its small haunches, ears up, and then hopped off across the field beyond the pond. A light in the hut under the yard trees shone like a red-gold star.

Why wasn't he asleep, this cowherd here? Why did he look at Ignat so keenly? This pale, blue-faced, yellow-headed herd boy who opened the door of the roomy warm hut? Over the table was suspended a lamp.

In the near corner stood an oil picture in a frame, St. Nicholas in a strawberry-colored mantle with a purple beard. A small pig walked across the sticky dirt floor, crunching something in its teeth. Behind the partition near the stove were young calves, brown and yellowish-white. They were still awake, their snouts with wide, tender, rosy-moist nostrils leaned upon the top partition board, staring with their bland eyes, urinating in thin straight light streams. They smelled of wet cow fur and warm cow's milk, with a heat almost intestinal. Long after, Ignat remembered this smell, simple and soothing. And there, in the midst of it, the old man, his own father. On the bed near the partition, the old man sat, dangling his pale, hairy legs in their thinnish blue breeches. He was a little bald and thin now, nearly a skeleton. Placing his large hands impressively on his knees, and shutting his blind eyes, he turned his face to the icon, whispering.

"He's a little touched," explained the herd boy, quietly, as he stared at Ignat. "He's got mighty aged here."

Hearing the voice and feeling someone's presence, the old man threw back his head, still more stately in his aged dignity, showing his thin nose, drawn with leanness.

"God bless you, God bless you," he murmured.

Uncovering his cropped head, bundled still by the

service muffler, but forgetting to greet his father, Ignat turned to the boy, "Is Lubka in the house?"

"In the house, yes. She's in the house," the boy answered hurriedly. "A city merchant's come to see her."

Ignat replaced his cap, left the hut and went up the hill, through the orchard. He walked rapidly toward the house, sinking in the drifts, and lurched across the greenish shadows of the house garden. And there, through the small window of the side hallway, he saw his wife.

Suddenly, a muffled bark of a dog came from behind the wall of the house. He jumped back and stood dead still, pressed against the wall.

IV

Lubka set the smoking samovar to boil in the dim corridor. By the light of a candle, burning low in its green-copper stick on the window-sill, she took up a needle and some socks. She seemed stout now, a pretty, black-eyed woman, with full breasts softly rounding in a red blouse, a white kerchief on her head, the wide part in her black hair retreating beneath its folds.

Two large shadows, one rising blurred, the other much more sharply, fell from her onto the wall, stretching from the candle to the ceiling. As Ignat came up to the window, Lubka was gazing thoughtfully at the sock, her head tilted to the side. From the darned heel,

155

she carefully drew out a scrolled silver soup-spoon. A spotted pointer, dappled with white and brown, stirred on a silk carriage cushion in a corner of the sitting-room, suddenly barked in a rich basso, jumped up, clawed along the parquet floor, and burst into the hallway. Lubka, startled, looked up, lively and concerned. She looked toward the door leading from the hallway into the sitting-room. Then, her hand against her cheek above the candle in the window, she flattened her face against dark pane.

"Who's there?" she demanded, loudly, her voice clear and authoritative. A little anxiously, however, she opened a small pane, then another, and looked out the opened square into the chilled light air.

The night, settling over the dead white world, over the villages now long asleep, over the estate frozen in silence, was crystallized at highest beauty. The spots of candle-light burned greenish on the garden snow. Lubka could not see the moon, but when she lifted her head, she saw its pale reflection on the branches of the pines. Beyond the tree trunks spread the white of the open yard, and the fresh twinned tracks cut into it by the merchant's sled were already frozen hard. She lowered her black brows, a strange anxiety spreading through her, a feeling of the presence of a man in the dark. She waited for an answer. Then she shut the little window and went into the sitting-room to set the table.

A SIMPLE PEASANT

In the large, chill drawing-room, the furniture stood helter-skelter, many straight chairs, and many stuffed easy arm chairs. Against the wall near the door to the hall stood a piano. The tall doors opening into the adjoining room were closed. Between the doors and the porcelain stove in the corner hung a blackish, full-length portrait, its paint peeling inside its gold frame. The table near the windows was lighted by a ceiling lamp suspended on chains.

The merchant had come from the city to see about the cutting of the Miliutin wood, which he had bought for timber. The buyer was spending the night in the manor house. He was a heavy-set man with an iron-gray beard, and small, black, cross-eyes. He opened the upper hooks of his full Romanoff pelt coat, displaying the sheepskin lining curling over his chest. Stepping quietly in his black felt boots, he walked around the room, idly, examining the furniture, the chiffoniers, the bronze horse under its glass bell on the marble mirror mantel. Near the stove a mouse was fussing, straining to pull through a small crack in the floor a large piece of half-chewed candy. The merchant gazed calmly at the mouse's struggles. The pointer, its attention, too, attracted, frisked and barked, and the merchant, with a half-smile of pleased interest, listened to the echo through the big house, an echo ringing on the copper strings of the piano. He strolled over and lifted the piano cover, and experimentally thumbed at the keys. . . .

"Nice here, in your place," he said to Lubka, as she went in and out of the room to the samovar in the corridor. "Quiet."

"Dull," said Lubka, with a small smile.

She set the table, brought out a small jar of green preserves, a salt bowl in which the salt was half bread crumbs, a plate with a slab of pork, rainbow-rusty and stuck in a cottony congealed grease, and a bottle of vodka, the glass bottle rimey from the frost.

"Why don't you find yourself some fun?" asked the buyer, hinting, with habit, at what one usually hints.

"Maybe I should," answered Lubka, vaguely, in her habitual carefree way.

There was none of the old liveliness in her tone. She had become quieter, she spoke less, plainly and more crudely, inured to squabbles with workers and losing her gloss of gentry manners. Thanks to the gift which is natural with women like her—not to give voice to anything superfluous—Lubka, with all her limitations, nevertheless gave the impression of being pretty wise.

When she brought in the samovar, raising it high in front of her, the buyer squeezed behind the table, edging along the new Viennese divan without once removing his cross-eyes from her breast. She looked sideways at him and, unhurriedly, with an air of apparent indifference, walked away from the table and stood, as if warming herself, against the cold stone of the fireplace. The merchant pushed back the sleeves of his fur coat and took a knife in his left hand, the fork in his right. Lubka noticed that, too. "A lefty," she thought. "I bet he's a fast one." The pointer, on the floor, again barked huskily, peering out into the hall, and Lubka listened anxiously.

"Who is he barking at?" asked the merchant, his nostrils expanding after the drink. "How that racket carries in here!" he added. "A regular organ this, not a house."

"That's that drunkard, I bet, the husband of our herdswoman," said Lubka. She smiled contemptuously. "There is so much fun around here. . . . God help us!"

The buyer cut off a piece of pork and carefully smeared on mustard.

"You don't say."

"So help me God," said Lubka. "She's been running around here with one fellow. But she won't turn down nobody. Of course, her man is roaring mad. I don't want to say anything, but I tell you there's going to be trouble."

"Well, did she find still another sweetie?"

"Plenty," said Lubka, thinking not of the herdswoman but of herself and of her own lover, the tailor

159

from Shatilovo who was madly jealous of her and continually threatened to kill her.

She glanced occasionally at the window. The frosty glass shone greenish in all its squares. Through the glass, the garden was blurred and faint in the snow. The merchant munched on, reflectively. Lubka yawned weakly and spoke again.

"The frost is going to be awful. Just stick your nose out and you'll freeze to death."

"That's right," said he, and looked at the dog which lay contentedly with its snout on its paws. "Whose dog is that?"

"That's the young one's—Nikolai Kuzmich's," she said. "I'm sick of her. She can't live in the yard, she's too delicate. She's too thin-skinned. Got to give her a bath twice a week; killing myself with the beast. He's a strange fellow."

"A damn fool, too, I might add," said the buyer.

"Fool or not, that's not my woman's business to judge," said Lubka, thinking that such a modest answer would please the city visitor. "But the truth is, he ain't much use, and he doesn't live at home. He writes about that dog in every letter, though. Worries over it."

"You been living here long?"

"Long! The seventh year, I guess."

"I suppose—contented?"

"Well, not bad. I'm the boss here, you know. Nobody to tell me. They ain't never here, the rest of them."

"Your husband in the army, eh?"

"In the army."

"Never done any fighting, I bet."

Lubka laughed, holding her hands behind her back as if warming them. "They have luck, the devils," she said.

"I bet his time's up soon, though?"

"That's the trouble. Too soon. He wrote and threatened: 'I'm going to drink myself to death!' What's that to *me*? '*You*'ll be the one lying in the gutter,' I told him," said Lubka, repeating the words she often told her tailor. "And he is jealous, too. I'm sick and tired of his love. He used to yell at me, 'I'll kill you,' and what then?—one soft word from me and he crawls all over the place. Well, he might kill. Even so. Sometimes I do get kind of scared, nights especially, when the dogs bark. I get kind of scary."

"You have a right to make a complaint," said the buyer. "The times are over when they could smack you down just like that."

He finished all of the pork, cutting around the fuzzy grease. He finished the rest of the vodka. His eyes became oily and he opened his heavy fur coat. Hiccoughing, he took out of his pocket a red packet of tobacco, a reed mouthpiece, a little book of papers, and carefully blew off a leaf. In his stubby fingers he rolled a thick cigarette.

"When did you get married?" he asked, smiling and puffing with enjoyment.

"Four years ago."

"No children?"

"No."

"How's that? I supposed you were strong, beautiful."

"Terribly beautiful," said Lubka, flattered, but smiling with contempt. She began to lie. "I don't suppose that's my fault. I want children myself. He must be sick or something. That ain't my fault. That's why he's sore. That's why he's cross. When I was young I was nobody's cold potato. I'd bite him black and blue and he would work hard . . . but no result . . . mean lot, a woman's," she wound up.

The merchant stared at her with narrowed eyes. He inhaled deeply, sending the smoke to the ceiling.

"Ye-es, that's right, all right," he said, not knowing what he was saying. "Say, why do you hide yourself behind the stove all the time?"

With artful simplicity, Lubka said: "Well, where should I be standing? This is my place."

"Sit down here at the table," said the merchant. "You'll get warmer here. Don't play so coy, I don't mind you."

"Well, if you don't mind, I'll sit by," she said, with a playful modesty, and took a chair at the table.

She realized that the merchant was growing uneasy, not knowing how to begin. He reclined on the divan, sighed at times, heaved at others, shut his eyes, and smiled darkly, and stared heavily at her breasts and her hair. His eyes, by turns, were glazed and bright. Pretending to notice nothing, Lubka lowered her eye-lashes, drank weak tea with lemon and modestly wiped her wet dark-downed upper lip with the tip of her headkerchief. The man sighed, still noisier, and, suddenly, without looking at her, hastily began unbuttoning with his thick awkward hands the bosom of his blue flannel shirt, under which it seemed he still wore an undershirt. He unbuttoned the undershirt, too, and groped inside, pulling out, at last, a wallet. Lubka moved a thin slice of lemon with her fingers, took it from the edge of her saucer, put it into her mouth and began to suck it, wrinkling her face out of all proportion, with the air of sensing only one thing, the sharp sourness of the citron. She noticed instantly that the wallet was very thick and worn, and her quick glance took in the swollen wad of banknotes which the merchant removed from the leather case. Peeling off one old note, repaired with gummed paper, he put back the others, shoving the wallet once more deep into the interior of his clothes.

He cupped his right hand over Lubka's.

"How's that, huh?" he asked.

Lubka calmly looked at the ten-ruble note, then shifted her warm gaze to him.

"You hear me?" he repeated, crudely.

She took up the bill, silently, and shoved it into the pocket of her jupe, and, crossing her arms, leaned upon the table, gazing at the man in continued silence. The merchant, not knowing what to do or say, seized her right hand and tugged playfully at the ends of her fingers. They felt clammy and chapped beneath his own. She pulled her hand free and, also not knowing exactly what were the words for the moment, asked, "Why didn't you finish the pork?" She took up a piece from the plate, and put it into her mouth.

"I like it," she said. "It's good. Especially when you fry it." And added, with a laugh, "Here it is Lent, and here we are gobbling away." After a silence she added, carelessly, "Well, we'll roast in hell, anyway."

"For what?" asked the merchant.

"For everything. Our place is in hell. The old people say that a peasant never makes a saint. It's only the priests and the bishops get the wings."

Suddenly she straightened up from the table and said resolutely:

"What do you say? Let's go."

A SIMPLE PEASANT

Ignat, standing in the snow, had long since lost the feeling of his legs. His head was like a frozen stone. His coat felt thin and icy. At first he had wiggled his toes in his army boots and jerked his shoulders in the cold. But later he paid no attention at all to the fact that the last vestiges of heat within him were centered, throbbing, in his breast. His lips were wooden, the ends of his muffler, his eye-lashes and moustache, were stiff with frost.

He paid no heed to time. He was lost in the morbid will to see his suspicions confirmed. From somewhere came a cockcrow. The night was passing. The paling moon sank westward. The three belt stars of Orion, like three silver buttons, glittered, paling, toward the horizon. The shadows of the peasants' hovels fell half across the yard. In the frosty quiet even the sound of the chickens stirring in their coops beside the huts seemed small and clear. From the stables came the crunching sound of the merchant's horse, still busy at his oats, and then the heavy movement of the animal's body as it lay down later with a sigh. Facing the sitting-room window, there was a bench at this side of the house half sunk in the snow beneath a garden fir tree. The snow creaked and crackled under the most careful step. Holding his breath, Ignat dragged himself to the bench and stood upon it. And pushing his head between the thick branches of the fir, he became oblivious of everything except the inside of the room—this appalling woman, speaking and smiling, and the man alone with her in the house at this late hour.

But time went on and nothing happened. Lubka was sitting down now at the cluttered table. . . . The man was pulling something from his bosom—but what? Ignat strained his eyes but could not see. The samovar, the dishes, all were in his way. Lubka rose, leaned on the table, edged over to the man, and through the unbuttoned slit of her dress Ignat saw her underskirt. Suddenly a terrible silence filled the world. There was only the mad beating of Ignat's heart. But at the same instant Lubka straightened up, and strode across the room toward the door leading farther inside the house, the man moving after her. And now, with no other thought in his mind, Ignat jumped off the bench and ran lightly under the firs to circle the house and enter it from the rear. The orchard below the house lay buried in snow. Ignat had noticed when he came through the garden that there were piles of cut wood between it and the house. In the woodpiles, he knew, there must be an axe. He ran to the nearest pile and feverishly, scratching his hands against the icy twigs and branches, rummaged for the familiar rusty tool with its worn slivery handle.

The merchant touched at the pocket of his fur coat to make sure his revolver was still there, and stepped into the hall with Lubka, groping behind her in the dark.

"Don't fall," she said. "There's wood there for the stove." And, stepping over the twigs, he smelled the pleasant bitter scent of the fresh-cut branches.

Lubka stopped, explaining: "This is our back way." She felt along the wall and opened the door into a large, unoccupied room, very cold, redolent of hams, and moonlit through its two small windows with still unfrozen upper panes. The room was half dark, yet the merchant noticed the hams hanging from the ceiling, a tub of smoked pork, a separator, a bicycle with its weakly glistening nickel parts, and pots dimly showing on the floor against the wall. A wooden bed without a mattress, with only one pillow and no pillow case. Backing toward the bed, Lubka again warned the man, in a whisper, confidentially suitable to the moment:

"Careful! Don't fall in the butter!"

She stood backed against the bed, awaiting him, her position frank and passive, to make it easier for the man to throw her. And, at her low husky tone, he instantly lost himself. She was still whispering something with a rich tremor in her voice, but he no longer heard—seizing and pressing her heavy body to him, he pushed her to the bed, nearer and nearer until her calves came close against the frame. The bed pressed hard against her knees, and Lubka, who resisted only weakly, fell back, wordless. She felt the pain from the pressure of his watch and chain and with one hand pushed aside his thick soft beard, with the other tightly gripping his index finger with its heavy gold ring. She felt the sweet torture filling her body, waves of relaxed power, and, as if in anger, bit into the hairs of his beard which covered her mouth. With both her hands she embraced and pressed him to her, clutching now the wrinkled bull-like neck, the tousled head. . . .

But, suddenly, this head began to drag slowly from under her arm, down the length of her body. Her body was lighter. But her legs hurt from the strangely shifted burden. She raised up on her arms. The merchant slumped heavily to the floor. He gasped and fell backwards, making a thud as the back of his head hit the boards. She jumped off the bed and tried to pull him to a sitting posture. But the man gasped as if in dying agony, whistling in his throat, his body with its ballooning stomach, enormous, cumbrous as a corpse. Fear chilled her.

With trembling hands she tore at the collar of his flannel shirt, pulling off the buttons, loosening the belt with its silver buckle. She took the pillow off the bed and threw it on the floor. She ran through the hall, lit a candle, shoved a towel into a pail of water and rushed back, the candle light in the hall falling upon rats scurrying off in all directions. Placing the light on the bed, she covered the forehead and the up-rolled eyes of the man with the towel, staring in horror at the mountainous bulk rising before her, at the open folds of his pelt coat, and at the white towel, now half covering his bluish face, its black beard thrusting upward. Suddenly, like a clap of thunder, she heard the slam of a door. She stood like a stone when the soldier towered in front of her. He seemed immense, to reach to the ceiling. In one hand he held his cap, in the other he clutched an axe. He took one step toward Lubka and shifted the handle in his palm. She caught, controlled the instant, and pinned him to the spot with her voice.

"All right. I did it," she said. Her words piled out. "Finish him off, quick! Now we can be rich. We'll say that his stroke killed him. Quick!"

Ignat looked at her suddenly drawn face, at the wide, fixed, black eyes, the red blouse and the full, fleshy arms—and with a terrific drive smashed the blunt head of the axe into the damp towel.

VI

When the cocks crowed the third time a lamp was already burning in the peasant quarters and a stove was crackling cheerfully. The cook, yawning lazily, sat on a bench against the stove, warming herself, and, without blinking, gazed into the hot multi-colored flame, and called Fedka. Fedka, the merchant's driver, was still asleep above the stove, in spite of his orders to hitch up early. The lad, still groggy from his slumber, let himself painstakingly down from above the stove, ladled out cold water from the tub, washed, peasant-like, around his mouth and piggish snout, tore briefly at his thick matted hair with the cook's wooden comb, made the sign of the cross toward the icon in the corner, coughed, squeezed himself behind the table, ate a pot of hot potatoes, poured a heap of salt on the bare boards in front of him, and bolted a huge slab of bread, importantly buried himself in all his coats, belted and buckled himself tightly round the middle, lit a pipe, and briskly squeaking over the frosty snow in his boots —stiff as wood and ginger-colored from wet-stains— swinging a smoky candle-lantern, set forth to hitch the horse.

The roosters in the barn yard left off their early racketing. Night mingled with day. The objects in the yard stood out with growing morning clearness. In the yard and upon the roofs, the snow lay deep and icy blue. The air was sharp as ether. In the thick green foliage of the frozen firs, the rooks were stirring and calling. In the west, the night still lingered, holding its mystery. The low moon hung dead over the sullen horizon, over the blurred slope beyond the snowy valley of the river. Fedka opened the barn doors and set the lantern on a ramshackle old carriage bemired by the hens and covered with dust. He seized the cold shafts of the merchant's small painted sled near-by and dragged its iron runners along the frozen earth, through the darkness, over the threshold outside to the pale morning light. He then took the horse collar from its wooden pin in the stone wall, pulled the harness out of the sled and strode along in the snow banks by the straw-packed windows of the stall where the merchant's horse was standing. In the dark, the stall seemed warm and earthy, smelling of the horse, its fresh manure and the sweet, left-over hay. The horse, gray with the loosely sifted snow upon its back, turned its head toward the light when it heard the sound of the door and neighed once, lightly. Fedka came up and the animal playfully lowered its head. The driver brought the bit close, and the colt curved its thick neck down, shaking its head suddenly and hitting Fedka in the chest, refusing to take the bit. Finally, with a show of force, Fedka pushed the bit between the animal's yellow teeth, and then turned aside and wiped his hands on the colt's tail, doing, at the instant, two jobs at the same time, wiping his hands and untangling the long twisted hairs of the tail, straightening it out. He then led the horse to the water trough.

Out of the quiet house, suddenly, rushed a dog, the

white and brown spotted pointer. Off the front steps it leaped, barked madly and then, like an animal lost, made two huge circles in front of the steps and rushed back into the house, darkly tranquil at this early hour, its windows dead and snow-covered.

Fedka looked after the dog in astonishment, but the horse was tugging toward the water. The animal pressed its nose on the icy film of the trough, broke it, and a light mist of steam rose above it. The colt gratefully flattened its velvet lips upon the surface and, sniffing, drew in slowly. It stopped, chewed on the icicles a moment, slightly turning its head to Fedka, while the driver stood by good-naturedly, whistled a note or two encouragingly, looking full into its large light eye and watching the clear water drops trickling from its lips.

"That's good," he said. "That's good now. You can't drink enough to last you a lifetime, anyway." He led the horse back to the sled. It had become entirely light now. In the garden, hidden in the leafless hedges, one could hear the chirping of the sparrows. The dull sky over the garden began to turn a reddish orange. The moon, tinged with red, set behind the white roofs of the village. Fedka hitched the horse, straightened the lines and, holding them in his hand, jumped for the seat as the colt, in a playful dash, suddenly jerked ahead. Fedka leaped after the sled, landing in it on the run, and cut the horse's mouth with the tight-reined bit. To warm up the animal, he drove across the rising hill and dashed through the fields to the gaily brightening east.

But the colt, no longer quite so light and frisky, tired soon. Having made about a verst and a half, and his face burning with the sharp head-on wind, Fedka swung around widely and jogged slowly on back to the house. Very sedately he entered the yard, driving up to the main front entrance, and suddenly he opened his eyes wide and pulled on the reins. The woman cook, wailing loudly, was running from the front steps toward the servants' quarters, her face haggard in the early sunlight. On the steps, at the threshold of the house, sat a man in a military coat, rough muffler tied around his chin and throat, his cropped head bared in the cold. Bending over, he was scraping up the fresh loose snow from the steps, with his right hand, and daubing it at his temples.

> *—Translated from the Russian by*
> *Morton Kent and Whit Burnett.*

ON THE GREAT ROAD

PARASHKA'S father lived on the great Novosilsk road. Wishing to keep away from the gentry, Ustin had chosen a piece of land that was till then uninhabited. Seas of rye poured in billowy fields around his farm-yard and merged in the vast Russian steppe. Two solitary scrub oaks stood in the rye outside the yard; shallow gullies receded from it into the distance, overgrown in summer with white flowers. Beyond the great road, one could see a small wood of oaks in the midst of the rye. Farther on was the village—the ancient free village of Bayevo—but this was wholly hidden by the billowy fields of rye. Many travelers passed along the great road. The tracks they left and the ruts, crisscrossing, stretched endlessly and were lost in a fine, tangled maze.

Ustin had long been a widower—it was rumored that he had killed his wife out of jealousy. He depended for his living not on tilling the soil like a peasant but on lending money. He sowed just enough land for his own use, around the scrub oaks and above the gullies. His cows were a poor lot, but he owned fine horses. His house had been managed first by his mistress, a widow, then by a beggar-woman, later by his elder daughter, Evgenya. But he soon got rid of Evgenya, who was unlike him and distasteful to him, and replaced her with a working man, the elderly and somewhat crack-brained Volodya. Ustin absented himself a great deal, and the barefoot, taciturn Parashka was left to grow up alone.

One day—she was then in her fourteenth year, and it happened in the summer just after Evgenya had moved to Bayevo—an immense flock of sheep was being herded along the great road, a frequent occurrence: a merchant would buy one or two hundred head at one fair and have them driven to another, hiring for the purpose several tramps with an overseer in charge. The summer sunset was fading, far away behind the farmhouse. In anticipation of her father's arrival from town, Parashka sat on the threshold and gazed at the vanishing evening meadows and down the long stretch of the empty road. In a dense, dirty gray mass the sheep slowly shuffled past her, making low indeterminate sounds by their movement and breathing, and exuding an odor of fleece and fodder, steppe grass and wormwood. Behind them came the dogs with their red tongues hanging parched and dusty from the day's journey, and a tall ragged youth walking beside a ragged old man, and last of all, astride a white, hook-nosed Kirghiz horse, whip in hand, a cap pushed back over the nape of his neck, rode a young merchant.

"How do you do, my beauty?" said the old man, stepping away from the sheep. "Please do a stranger a favor. Ask your father for a match."

She looked at him for a long time without answering. He wore no hat, but the shreds of one hung on his smooth staff. He pressed his shiny hands down on the staff to restrain their trembling, and breathed with difficulty. In his tattered reddish overcoat, barely covering his naked body and belted with a strip of cloth, and his worn shoes, greenish gray and shaggy, his face deathly pale with puffy eyes, he presented a fierce appearance, but in his hoarse voice there was goodness, weariness. The gray hair was visible on his chest, which betrayed the beating of the heart under it.

"Father isn't at home," Parashka replied after sharp scrutiny.

"Just as I thought, just as I thought," said the old man. "Life goes on, an' you're growing up. 'Evening's a quail, a speckled quail, that keeps calling through the long night, the dark night.' What's one to do, then, my beauty?"

The youth also came up to her, followed at a slow trot by the man on horseback, who, in the manner of riders of the steppe, pressed his feet in the stirrups under the belly of the thick-chested Kirghiz horse, which appeared hungry and heated, tossing its large head back and twisting its neck. They gave the old man a mocking glance—they knew his way of speaking—and looked more attentively at Parashka. The youth was tall and slender, with sloping shoulders, and a round feline face; he wore a convict's cap. The man on horseback was very swarthy and lean but broad-shouldered; he had gleaming eyes.

"I know her father," he said, looking down from his saddle at Parashka, at her small feet, her tanned shoulders and dirty chemise. "A rich rogue. Just go in and have a look on the oven shelf, or behind the icon," he added gruffly.

Without taking her eyes off the Kirghiz horse—a short, sturdy, yet light-footed beast, tossing its heavy head and gnawing with yellow teeth at the spittle-flecked bridle—Parashka sprang up from the threshold; then she ran into the house and returned with a box of matches. Meanwhile, the merchant had dismounted from the old, dry, dirty Cossack saddle, and stretched his short legs. The youth walked away, his eyes fixed somewhere upon the fields. The merchant took the matches and, in silence, also walked away, leading his horse toward the flock of sheep, which had come to a stop with lowered heads. Parashka was to remember always his dust-covered coat, his glossy breeches thrust into broad-topped boots with narrow toes, his embroidered shirt with its dirty collar, and, above all, his face, which, as if dusted with powder, was covered with bluish-tipped pimples, and his swarthy cheeks that showed a sparse growth of stiff beard, scarcely less sparse than the stiff jet-black hairs above the corners of his mouth. As he walked away, he turned to glance at her again, and astonished her with the beauty of his hard eyes. The old man, who apparently had noticed this, said in a strange tone as he also took his leave: "Well, that's how we live.—Good-bye, and thank you, my beauty. Remember what a terrible old barefoot man once told you. This merchant-thief has it in him to ruin you. Don't waste any looks on such as he. . . ."

And then, on the field beyond the great road, where the flock of sheep stopped to rest for the night, there flamed for a long time, in the darkening blue of the evening, a hot yellow campfire. It grew late, and her father had not yet come home. As she sat on the threshold, Parashka could hear the man Volodya at his milking in the shed, but she did not take her eyes off the fire. "Evening's a quail"—she remembered the old man's words—and, aware of a sweet longing they awakened, she looked into the dark night and imagined she saw the quail, which was calling—calling in the boundless sea of rye. The fire flamed redder and redder —and he, this dark-eyed merchant, who had it in him to ruin her, was still there, very near. At last, the measured, comforting sound of her father's cart became audible. She jumped up, ran inside the dark house and, lying down, pretended to sleep. Her father drove up to the door, shouted to Volodya, then entered and hung something up on the wall. The drowsy flies in the sieves and strainers near the stove began to hum.

"Father," called Parashka in a low voice.

"Well, dear?" her father replied in a whisper.

"Who's this barefoot old man that comes round?"

"If you took your shoes off, you'd be barefoot too!"

"He's not really barefoot. He's got boots on—what's left of them."

"That means he's drunk 'imself to pieces. But where did you see 'im?"

Parashka told of the passers-by, but she said nothing of the old man's parting words.

"That means they were driving Balmashev's flock," he said, without paying much attention to her story as he moved a horse's bridle from one hook to another. "Yes, yes, I see, the campfire's still going—"

"Why was his horse all blood?"

"Whose horse?"

"The overseer's. The horse's chest is all red scabs."

"That all comes from its being a Kirghiz horse," her father replied. "It's a mean, very fierce breed. That's the bad blood coming out. An' did he have a brand on 'im?"

Parashka thought a while. "What may a brand be?"

"It's a kind of a stamp—like letters burnt into the leg —to make you see it's no common horse but a Kirghiz. —Well, go to sleep, sleep, if you've already had supper," he added. "As for me, I'm going into the pantry to have a bite."

And, having opened the window, he went into the other part of the house. Through the window she could see the night sky dotted with pale stars; and the fresh air drew in, mingled with the smell of the dying campfire. And so, troubled by this smell that reminded her of something, and at the same time listening to her father scolding Volodya in a low voice outside the window, she fell asleep in that mood, half pain, half allurement, that unknown passing travelers awaken—a mood of enchantment at the vague thought of him who had it in him to ruin her, of the young merchant who could bear her away into the remote distance. . . .

Two years went by, and now a third had come. In some ways Parashka had changed a great deal. Gradually she took her place in the management of the house. She carried all sorts of heavy things, lifting pots and pans from the oven, straining her young body; and she milked the cows and mended her father's clothes. Yet her inner nature had changed but little.

One summer she was seized by a passion for the village. She began to adorn herself, to pay visits to her sister Evgenya, to join with other girls in the round dances, to sing and skip about with them, pretending to be a lively piece. Then she dropped it all, again felt a stranger to the village, to the girls, to Evgenya. Evgenya also visited the farmhouse. She lived the life of a soldier's wife; she had no children; she was not afraid of her widowed father-in-law. Both the girls were taciturn, but otherwise they were different in every way. No one, indeed, would have thought of taking the attractive and outwardly calm Parashka for Evgenya's sister. Evgenya was strong, broad-shouldered; she drew her eyebrows together when she looked at you, at the same time pursing her lips. To the delicate oval of Parashka's shy virginal face her sister's short aggressive face with its high cheek bones presented a startling contrast.

Only Parashka's father was close to her. Her love for him increased with each year. But it was not a simple, tranquil love.

She loved her father timidly, with that poignant feeling that daughters so often have for widowed fathers. To take her mother's place, to be his housekeeper, to look after him, to drag pots out of the oven for him —this was her greatest pride and joy. At times this joy was poisoned with pain—for she would suddenly remember some mistress who had once managed her father's house. In that terrible affair between her father and mother, of which she understood little although she had heard from Evgenya some incoherent whispers even during her childhood, she generally took her father's side. But at times she was troubled by doubts: had he really been in the right? And then it would seem to her that there had never been in this world a person better or more beautiful than her mother. Parashka saw but little of her father, and she understood him even less; she always felt shy and embarrassed in talking with him. And he did not have the reputation of being a simple or easy-going man. With his clean-cut, regular features, his spare form, and his small bronze beard and keen green eyes, he reminded old servants in the big country houses of a mounted Circassian guard who had once lived with the gentry. Yet there was also something of the peasant in his cautious manners and his clumsy boots, in his thick curls, which he brushed to one side, in the coarse shirt and rough sleeveless peasant's coat which he wore. He was shrewd and courteous, even good in a fashion, but everyone was a little afraid of him. He was exceedingly judicious. People came to him from the hamlets and villages for assistance, which he never refused. He listened attentively, shook his head, constantly pushing back the bronze locks from his forehead. He looked searchingly at visitors but not sternly, nodding assent, never interrupting them with so much as a whisper. He charged only a moderate rate of interest. But, after all, he lived by lending money, and such people always arouse a measure of fear.

Parashka had grown thin. In her face there appeared an elusive likeness to her father, such as one may sometimes come to see in daughters who love their fathers, even where at first glance no likeness is apparent. They had in common the faculty of concealing much, of withholding themselves, of receiving similar impressions. For example, they were both considerably disturbed by the sight of an immense gypsy caravan going down the great road in the autumn toward the valleys of the south.

"When I was a youngster I once ran away to follow the gypsies," Ustin said one day, with a grin.

"Well, what happened? Did you change your mind?" Parashka asked.

"Yes, I changed my mind. It's the proper thing to do, daughter," he said, no longer smiling. "One shouldn't do things in a hurry—"

"An' why not?"

"Well, never mind"—he did not answer at once and evaded her glance. "The fact is, the blood sometimes comes into your eyes, and makes trouble—"

She understood him, shrank back, and was silent.

There were other things around her that affected Parashka beside her father's mysteriousness—his past, his journeys, and his cares, about which he never confided in anyone. In the autumn and the winter she slept a great deal. In the summer sometimes she did not sleep for three nights together. Her favorite spot was the threshold, where she would stand by the hour, her head turned to one side. Somewhere into the distance, toward some happy land, went the passing travelers. An itinerant beggar in skullcap and cassock strode along with rapid step, swinging his tall staff, looking boldly and eagerly ahead of him, his sun-streaked, tangled hair brushing his shoulders. She followed him with her steady gaze, although she was afraid of tramps, afraid when they turned in toward the house to ask for alms. At a jog trot, the three horses stumbling and snorting, a country gentleman's jaded *troika* passed down the middle of the road. The much-traveled look of the dust-covered carriage, the sound of the creaking springs, awakened a longing in her—indefinable desires. When she saw a flock of sheep go by, she fixed her eyes avidly on the drivers, and remembered the evil foretold. But it was at the endless seas of rye that billowed away beyond the great road, toward the southeast, into the tormenting distances of the steppe, that she gazed most often.

As for love—to her it was no simple word. She had learned it early, and even while she was still a child it disturbed her. Once in the heat of a summer noon she saw sitting on the stones by her father's storehouse a poor drunken woman from Bayevo. She was on her way to the fair—to sell her sick bony nag standing near by. She had spread before her some matches with a tin of cheap tobacco; she smoked and smiled at Parashka, who was playing in the dust. "W-well, hasn't your father driven out his love-bird yet?" she asked in a secretive hoarse whisper. And Parashka always remembered this particular word and intuitively sensed its mysterious meaning. After that, whenever she happened to run into the house and see a woman on her father's knee, a sweet terror and shame overcame her. Later, from her sister and from the girls of the village she learned songs —all with a single theme—love. And she sang them, and inwardly they stirred her, especially one very old song: "And he fell asleep, asleep, my dear one, on a girl's arm, a muslin sleeve. . . ." All her companions were getting ready for one thing—for married life, for intimacy with their husbands. She too had begun early to be disturbed by a presentiment of this intimacy. Her sister would often say simply: "Father's a loose man, he's living with some woman again. If it costs me a hundred rubles, I'll find her out!" But not for a hundred rubles would Parashka have tried to find about her father's mistress, although she thought about her day and night.

One day shortly after her husband was called up for his army service, Evgenya came to the farmhouse. "Is father at home?" she shouted hoarsely, appearing at the frozen window. Then she entered and, seating herself on the bench, began to munch bread, and went on saying that she had just come in for a minute, all the while glancing at the tall lean peasant Volodya, who repeatedly came and went through the room. Fussing over some ropes and reins lying on the bench, he mumbled to Evgenya in a thick voice: "Why don't you take your coat off?" Parashka's sister slowly drew back her head, covered by a hempen kerchief: "I've just dropped in for a minute—" She wore bast shoes, and had on a red skirt of coarse wool and a rough bodice tightly fitted over her full breasts. A strong odor emanated from her—the odor of a robust healthy woman, of the smoke in a peasant's hut and of the rye bread which she was slowly munching. "Oh, why do I go on sitting here?" she exclaimed. And suddenly she rose and went resolutely out. But she did not turn her steps homeward; instead she went in the direction of the shed, where Volodýa had gone. Parashka rushed up to the door of the shed and stood there stock-still, her ear pressed to the keyhole. The minutes passed, and still there was no sound. But to Parashka it seemed that she heard everything, saw everything. . . .

As she took her mother's place in the house and became its mistress, she began to feel grown up, and at times carried on real conversations with her father. One summer evening he was sitting close to the small lamp, sorting the various smudged scraps of paper piled on the table, and taking others out of his bosom and the pocket of his peasant's coat. He was intent upon something and kept moving his lips. Then, with a stump of a pencil he began writing, leaning his chest against the table and pushing back his hair with his sleeve; he fidgeted a long time with the papers before setting down a figure. Parashka, sitting near the stove, worked at the spinning wheel; with her left hand she twisted the thread, while with the right she adroitly managed the spindle. She was good to look upon in her many-colored print dress, her head uncovered, her eyelids lowered; she herself became aware of this from the strange, affectionate glances which her father, raising his eyes from his work, from time to time cast at her. She seemed to sit calmly, lightly on the bench, her rounded knees slightly parted, gently pressing the pedal of the spinning wheel with the tip of the left foot and making it hum. "Father," she said suddenly, "were you always so handsome?"

"Eh, what?" he asked in a whisper, as was his habit. "Always. But why?"

"Why, then, didn't mother love you?"

"Who told you that?"

"Oh, I know," she said enigmatically.

He was silent. Then he began to hide the papers in his bosom and to fasten the hooks of his coat; he tossed his head, brushing the locks of hair back from his brow.

"There are some things you'd better not 'ave heard," he said in a low voice.

"They say—you killed her.—Why? For another woman?"

"And you needn't go into that either," he said quietly and simply. "Now, I don't pry into your affairs, do I?"

She reflected. "Why should you pry into my affairs? I'm all on the outside."

"Go on arguing!" he said. "You're just like her."

She flushed. "No, I'm like you—I'll never betray you for anyone in the world!"

"You will, daughter, you will—"

She recalled the merchant who had come with the

sheep, the summer evening, which seemed so remote now and so lovely, the old yellow-toothed fiery Kirghiz horse, his powerful chest with the stripes of dried blood. Then her father said in an even voice, as if he were reading from a book: "I'll never give you up until the proper time comes. It's for you, daughter, for you alone, that I work from morning till night. I'll wait until a good, handsome man turns up—"

"But you have a love-bird," she whispered.

"That's all nonsense, all nonsense," he answered warmly, without raising his voice. "All that needn't concern you. It's shameful to gossip with one's father about such things—"

She began to cry. He went up to her, put an arm around her head and kissed her hair. His thin skin flushed suddenly red, his green eyes burned brightly and tenderly. She managed to get a glimpse of them just as he turned and went out of doors, and she wept from a kind of incomprehensible joy, and even more incomprehensible sorrow. *Akh*, how could anyone be better and handsomer than her father!

She was low-spirited. But her arms and legs grew rounder, her small breasts rose higher, her hair became thick and glossier. When she bathed, she began to feel ashamed of her nakedness. Her sixteenth spring! Soon, soon she would be betrothed; matchmakers would arrive to interview her father; her right to love and to choose would be established—though, of course, she would never marry anyone. Her sister became franker with her—this gratified her vanity. She revealed the mysteries of love to Parashka, and said how eagerly she awaited the return of her soldier husband, how impatient she was growing. Parashka, too, felt a desire to talk about herself, her thoughts, her weariness. She also wanted to hint that she knew about Volodya.

Going with her sister to the door, she would stand a long time at the threshold. The cocks sang out—she heard them, shutting her eyes. The shadowy March mist drowsed above the gray snow of the fields—it seemed to her that she already heard in the mist the cawing of the first rooks. The muddy winter road ran off into the mist, and disappeared—it lured one on, drew one toward distant depths. There were tricklings of water; the hens stood under them and also drowsed —then suddenly grew restless and began to cackle through their heaviness. An excited panting dog, chained near the storehouse, played about gaily, with a simulated fierceness. Startled and trembling, Parashka would rush indoors again.

Only Volodya shared her solitude in the warm home. It was his fifth year with Ustin. Now he awakened only horror and repulsion in her—she had felt this way from the evening when Evgenya had gone into the shed to him. Yet she often stayed alone with him. She knew that he would never dare touch her—her father would have killed him—yet she thought about it. And the sweet agony of her secret thoughts became all the more intense because of the horror and repulsion. At a glance he was not bad-looking; he was no longer young, but he was well-built and lithe, like a young man of twenty. Sometimes she tried to talk with him about something which had no connection with the household—about the village, about girls, about young men. That would set him pondering. Sitting on a bunk, he would throw aside the rope he was twining, and keep turning the cheap cigar between his fingers. His grayish lean face bent forward so that a lock of gray hair fell across his low forehead, he seemed attractive. But he no sooner opened his mouth than he was transformed into a fool. No matter what subject she began the conversation with, he always brought it back to such questions as who lived where among the workmen and, above all, what wages each man was getting.

"He gets big money—" he would mutter, and as he muttered, his mustache would become slobbered.

When the south wind blew in spring, consuming the thawing snow, and she grew even more disturbed, he saw it and felt it. He would enter the house as if to attend to something, would hang up or take down a bridle and, deliberately lingering, would begin with some jest: "It's time to put the bit in order and bridle you, to lead you to the stallion." Whereupon she would laugh with a strange loudness. Or he would walk past her and give her an appraising scrutiny. She would meet his eyes with wide eyes, full of expectation. Another minute, it seemed, and she would be completely in his power. But no sooner had he stretched out his arms than her eyebrows trembled violently, her face became distorted with fear and flushed with anger. She would jump up and, with that sudden harshness with which girls so often stupefy men, would scream loudly, seizing anything which came to hand: "Just touch me! And I'll batter in your snout! I'll tell father as soon as he comes home! And there won't be the ghost of you left here, you devil!"

Spring came. The winds and the mists had consumed the gray snow; a softness hovered over the wet fields. Passion week ended, Easter eve followed. It was a dismal evening. Parashka and her father drove in a cart to the village church. The bare limbs of the trees on the edge of the village made a comfortless sound, while behind them in the treacherous twilight showed blue-white clouds, threatening rain and snow and giving the horizon a dour look. But in the icy wind which blew from under the clouds there was freshness, the aroma of spring. Parashka's face burned—from the wind and from her rouge and from an inward agitation—also from having washed and dressed herself up in clean clothes for the occasion, and from the excitement of riding in a new cart by the side of her rich and handsome father as he drove his well-fed horse along the road.

The broad village street was slushy; ice lay about in huge humps. In the village the evening seemed still more desolate, in the unfamiliar street along which the lights already shone from the poor but snug little houses. But even in these early lights, and in the flakes of snow which the wind suddenly swept the length of the street, strangely whitening its filth and its dark roofs—in all this, the spring holiday was evident. Half closing their eyes against the snow, Parashka and Ustin turned away with bowed heads. Now and then, Parashka glanced up furtively, and her heart grew faint with an incomprehensible joy at the sight of her father's dear face, his thin skin, grown more youthful looking in the wind, his shining snow-flecked beard and wet eye-lashes.

Suddenly someone shouted loudly at them: "Gone blind, have you? Drive a little more to the right, please!"

And on opening her eyes Parashka saw a tall horse and a carriage, high in front, and in the carriage—the raised collar of an overcoat, and the merchant, his face also turned away from the snow and the wind. He glanced at her—and instantly she recognized him.

"What makes you shout so?" Ustin replied with gaiety in his voice. "And tomorrow's Easter!"

"Sorry, Ustin Prokofitch," the merchant replied. "One can't see a thing—"

And the two vehicles parted company.

After a long silence, Parashka asked calmly, "Do you know him?"

"An' who doesn't know the rogue?" said Ustin. "He lived at Balmashev's farm. Now he's hatching a business of his own. He's hopping about like a thief, an' he wants to open up a shop in the village—"

Parashka put her dress in order, drew the shawl across her face, held her breath. Her heart thumped, her face grew serious. She accepted this chance meeting as something that had to happen; it did not even surprise her. What did surprise her was the lightness with which fate had so unexpectedly taken a turn.

During Easter week the merchant paid Ustin a friendly call. In the three years since Parashka had first seen him, he had not changed in the least; only his fiery eyes had become more restles. Even his clothes were the same, but this time the collar of his shirt was clean. She learned that his name was Nikanor; from his talk with her father she gathered that he was still uncertain of his future. Should he, or should he not, go to Rostov, where somebody was ready to hire him? He drank tea and vodka with his host. She did not try to grasp the meaning of his words, but merely listened to the sound of his clear voice. She did not raise her eyes. Dressed all in white and rouged, she sat in the corner and chewed sunflower seeds, pretending not to notice the visitor. For his part, he also avoided noticing her, or appeared not to notice. But when he took his leave, he stretched out a hand to her. She was not used to touching the hands of strangers, and reached out hers rather awkwardly—and grew pale. This handclasp gave her a strange pleasure, and made her flush with shame as if it were actually the beginning of their secret coming together.

After this he did not appear for a long time. For days on end she stood at the threshold, and impatiently awaited him with the persistent and unreasoning hope of adolescents. It seemed to her that he was under a compulsion, that he must at all costs come back and continue what he had begun, though she knew very well that he had begun nothing.

Let him but arrive—she thought—and I'll turn my back on him and go away. I'll show him that I have no need of him—

Almost an entire month had passed. May brought cold and rain—and still there was no sign of him. On the eve of St. Nicholas' day she looked for him especially, she knew not why; she was tormented by such a desire to see him that it seemed to her impossible it could go unfulfilled. That evening she went to bed early and wept so angrily and so bitterly as to drench the pillow, yet so silently that her father, who slept but a few feet away, did not even suspect her tears. He only heard her tossing and turning over, and from time to time asked her in a strange, agitated voice what troubled her and kept her from sleep.

The next morning her father went away somewhere. She looked at the windowpanes with rivulets of rain running down them; and suddenly she felt that she was no longer waiting for anything, no longer wanted anything, that it was a pleasant thing merely to rise, to clean the house, to build a fire in the stove, to attend to everyday matters. Toward evening she rigged herself out, stuck two dry cornflowers into her braid wound round her head, and thought of setting the samovar going.

The rain ceased. Everything was wet—the green of the road and the green of the rye fields, beyond which were moist blue walls of clouds casting their shadows upon everything. The samovar was boiling; its grating flamed red in the dark passageway. She stepped out of the house, with the smoke-blackened teapot in her hand, singing, "It is fearful to face the Judgment Seat, to receive the golden crown—" and coming in again waited for the samovar to boil harder. Just then Volodya came from the farmyard and crossed the threshold, bringing in a fresh smell of rain and musty wet cloth. He was about to approach her, aware of her yielding mood, when close to the door frame there appeared the head of a tall horse someone had driven up. Volodya walked straight on through the house, opened the door leading to the shed and disappeared, while Parashka, without raising her eyes, again went faint.

"How do you do?" said the merchant boldly from the threshold. "Seems I've come at the right time, just as you're about to have tea."

And, laughing, he took off his cap and shook it. His black peasant's coat was sleek from the rain. His swarthy face, with its look of being sprinkled with powder, was wet.

He did not speak now at all in the tone in which he had addressed her in her father's presence. She made no answer, and flushed. He was also silent for a moment—the cooing of the pigeons in a dark corner under the roof became clearly audible—then he walked up to her and, glancing at the samovar, asked, "Isn't your father at home?"

"No," she answered in a low voice as she bowed her head, upon which the cornflowers showed very blue.

"A pity," he said and struck his whip across his boot-leg. "So you're alone and making the best of it?"

"Yes, making the best of it," she replied, with a faint smile.

"Well, never mind. I'll run in again another time," he said. "Good thing I've got an excuse. Really, I don't feel a bit like myself. I've been dying to see you.

"You don't believe me?" he said, cautiously embracing her. "Well, I'm telling the truth. I fell in love with you the first time I saw you, the day I was driving the sheep. And then when I saw you in the village, I was so blinded I nearly drove the horse down into the ravine. I just felt that there must be a romance between us or I'd go to the devil!"

"I've heard such tales before," she answered with difficulty. "Let me go," she said coldly, pushing his arm away with her elbow.

But he did not release her. He knew that she had not yet heard such tales. He tightened his embrace and now spoke with genuine warmth: "May God cause me to die without absolution, if I lie! May He deny me the sight of my own father and mother—"

She was silent. It seemed to her as if she were on the verge of falling. He glanced furtively around him, then bent over her, found her lips and pressed her face back. The long, stolen kiss left them both breathless. Then, with a pretense of despair, he waved his arms and walked to the threshold.

"Now I'm done for!" he said, seating himself in his cart. "My peace is gone for ever—"

And swiftly he drove his tall horse across the bright

green grass; it loomed against the cloud whose shadow was already merging with the twilight.

Soon he had vanished from sight. Everything suddenly grew quiet, and it seemed to her as if, at first but a few steps away, a struggle was going on between two quail that kept calling to each other as they flew farther and farther off into the remote rye fields, beyond the little wood now barely visible. . . .

He came twice more, both times unseasonably. Ustin was at home. And she pretended not to notice him, while he talked with her father in a business-like fashion. Frustrated in her desire to see him face to face, if only for a moment, she moved about like one drunken. . . .

Evgenya's soldier husband returned. With his wife, his father, and his stepmother, he arrived on St. Peter's day at Ustin's house, driving a short light-bay horse, harnessed to a new cart, the wheels smeared with fresh brown tar. The soldier's father, a short-legged peasant with a black beard turning gray near the mouth, and a peculiarly jovial manner, had just wed for the third time; his wife was lame, she had insolent eyes and pointed youthful breasts. Everyone felt embarrassed on his account, but he himself was cheerful and garrulous, probably to conceal his own embarrassment. Ill at ease, they drank too much at lunch. They also ate too much, and kept pressing one another to take more of the various dishes. They talked nonsense, and again, with hits at the newly wed old man, in riddles and proverbs, each in turn interrupting the others. During the entire meal Parashka feared that at any moment a quarrel might break out, and she felt faint, as if overcome by fumes.

After lunch they drank tea and vodka just outside the house, on the green grass in the shade. All sense of shame lost, the soldier's drunken father went to their cart and returned reeling, with an accordion, which he thrust into his son's hands demanding that he play a dance tune. The soldier, with smutty face and uniform undone, sat on the bench near the table and rolled from side to side, every instant on the verge of falling. For a long time he could not grasp what his father wanted. Finally, he understood and abruptly, savagely began to play, "If only the hen would give birth to a bull—" The thrice-wed man thrust his hands under his black peasant's coat behind his back, and danced in a squatting posture, bending his knees low and beating a rhythm upon the ground with his boots. Clapping the palms of her hands together, his lame wife came forward and joined in, her goat-like breasts shaking up and down. Evgenya's face became rigid with sluggish spite. Ustin leaned his head upon an elbow propped on the table, his thin fingers thrust into his bronze locks, his teeth tightly set. An ill-natured smile had congealed in the corners of his lips. His eyes sparkled with a kind of morose joy.

"Daughter! Come here!" he shouted rather sternly, moving his eyebrows in such a way as to belie his tone. "Come here and kiss me!"

"You are drunk," Parashka answered. "I am ashamed to look at you!"

Her lips trembled. She turned on her heels and went off, out of sight of the house. There the sun, now low on the horizon, dazzled her. Two young doves, their wings flashing, flew down from the oaks and dropped amid the rye, into the shallow hollows overgrown with flowers. How quiet it was here after the din of the drunkards! The vast stretch of the rye fields in the light of the sunset was golden and serene, lovely to look upon. Parashka sat down by a hedge and gave full vent to her tears.

After she had wept a long time, she dried her tears and decided to return to the house and there, with her sister's help, to put an end to the indecency—to separate the drunkards, to remove the vodka and the samovar. Night had already come, strange and radiant. High up in the heavens, immense dull clouds appeared in ponderous piles—the heavens seemed vaster and more majestic than ever, and the moon shining in them seemed larger and more mirror-like. On the wide road, over the rye fields, shadows moved in great patches. The poles of the cart, which stood near the house, and the straw in it gleamed silvery. The soldier's father sprawled in the cart, wrangling with his drunken wife. An overturned bench lay near the table. A streak of light shone on the copper of the samovar where it stood to one side; a pool of spilt water shone dimly on the table, for someone had removed the samovar tap. Under the projecting eaves of the storehouse the panting dog on his chain was playing pranks, as if excited by the moon, now shining, now hidden. Parashka went into the house. Close to the lamp the soldier sat at the table, both elbows resting on it, holding up his stupefied head in his hands. He was muttering something. Drowsily and sullenly the flies buzzed in the sieves and strainers which hung on the wall near the stove. As for the soldier, he was talking to someone, boasting that as a man of importance he would be "assigned" to the service of some sort of *barin*, some man of standing like Yakov Ivanovitch. . . .

But where was her father? Where was Evgenya? Parashka turned, walked out into the passageway, and paused on the threshold. Now the high warm moon shone brightly amid the dull cloud masses. Just across the threshold, holding the reins in one hand and a whip in the other, stood the merchant, his tall horse, saddled, behind him. The moonlight gave his face a changed expression.

"Your dad's in fine shape—and full, oh my!" he said, with a smile, to Parashka, who was stunned with fright. "I just met him in the rye. Drunk?—well, you could squeeze the vodka out of him! He was saying, 'I'm off to the village!' and Evgenya was pulling him back."

Parashka was silent. The merchant dropped the reins, took her icy hand in his own strong hot one, and pushed her into the passageway. She moved back, leaning on him. She was dimly aware, over his shoulder, of the smoky-green strip of moonlight which fell through a hole in the roof into the darkness, as he pressed her against the cold stone of the wall and began kissing her face, whispering ardently between kisses: "Just wait, for God's sake, just wait—'Where, alas the day, when like an arrow we flew, when they burnt us with love, when they scorched us with flame.'—I've lost my senses over you! I'll take you away to Rostov. I'll marry you there. We'll settle on the steppe, in the Caucasus. We'll make thousands out of horses. You'll go finer than any dressmaker!"

She recalled him as he was when she first saw him—with the sheep and dogs, on his branded Kirghiz horse—and she put one arm around his neck, trembling from head to foot with happiness and tenderness, and hid her face against his breast. Then, abruptly, and resolutely, with both arms she embraced him. . . .

When she came to herself, she remained sitting for a

long time in a corner on the straw. The merchant tried to kiss her, to say something impetuously. She pushed him away, and violently shook her head, to show that she was not listening. He glanced furtively out through the passageway, and said rapidly that he would come again the next night, that she must meet him under the two oaks beyond the house, that he had something important to discuss with her.

"I'll come, I'll come," she replied.

"See that you don't fool me," he said, in a forced tone, as if he understood that she would not come.

She could hear the clink of the stirrup as he vaulted into the saddle, and the stamp of the horse's hooves impatient to start. She looked at the strip of moonlight, then lowered her eyes.

When the merchant, turning, said again to her, "See that you don't fool me," she suddenly saw framed in the little window of the door leading to the shed the cap and face of Volodya. There was as much horror in his eyes as if death herself had looked in. "And now it's all the same!" she thought. Her heart thumped so hard that breathing was difficult; her breasts rose and fell, and she pressed her hands against it. This did not prevent her from thinking clearly. What she thought was very simple: she was lost! And it was all so terrible, and so unexpected, as such things are in a dream!

Several days after the feast day, Ustin still went

about frowning. He was ashamed of his drunkenness. As for Parashka, she was weary from weakness: she felt broken and wanted to lie in bed from morning till night. But it was necessary to be up, to seem cheerful and calm, even to joke at dinner with her father and Volodya. From morning till night she thought of one and the same thing.

Ustin kept going off and coming back again. It seemed to her that if he had stayed at home and had not hurried away, if he had not upset her with his comings and goings, she could have got hold of herself and devised some way out, some means of saving herself. It was terrible to think that if he lingered at home and watched her closely, he might guess everything. But at times she desired, ardently desired, to have him understand; then somehow the whole thing would find some natural way of settling itself. It seemed to her that if only the days were rainy, gloomy, she could bear it all more easily. But they were bright now, sultry, and endless. The busy time in the fields was approaching; the heavy, dryish rye was ripening, yellowing—and there was no place to hide from the glare and the heat. After that strange feast day, which had destroyed the workaday routine of the farmhouse, the place had become, as it were, even more silent than usual; and a strained hush hovered over the house and over the bright yellow fields.

Day after day, she sat on the bench near the table in the hot empty house, observing the numberless flies with the tiny new ones on the hot dusty windowpanes. Volodya said nothing, but as always seemed preoccupied; he found all manner of trifling things to do out of doors and rarely came into the house. When he did enter, he acted as if nothing had happened; only he made no more amorous advances. What did it mean? It must be that he was waiting for some propitious moment and was hoping that this time he would not fail. Parashka smiled bitterly. The fool! It would be better if he told her father everything he had seen!

One day at noon, when a soft luminous haze hovered over the rye fields and the hot dusty road, and the high dazzling clouds were but faintly visible, a team of horses stopped before the storehouse. In the carriage sat a lady who, as Parashka knew, owed Ustin a great deal. She looked fatigued and worried; there was dust on her gray face. In a pensive tone, she began saying over and over the same thing—what a pity it was that she had not found Ustin at home. She lingered for an incredibly long time, looking about her. Then, screwing up her eyes, she began to examine Parashka's emaciated face, her transparent green eyes. "Are you well?" she suddenly asked.

Parashka answered simply and firmly that she was

well, but after the lady had taken her departure she spent an hour looking in the mirror as she sat on the bench by the window; she was shocked by her likeness to her father, and her heart grew faint with horror. She had changed a great deal—a child could see that—how had her father failed to observe it? But he would soon see it too; then he would grasp everything, all that had happened—and what then?

In her mind's eye she reviewed her whole short life. And she saw for the first time that she had never before even suspected the kind of enchantment she lived under, how much her thoughts centered around one thing, how many confused and captivating pictures of some remote happy city, of remote steppes and roads, her imagination held, how tenderly in her dreams she loved someone.—She now felt that by his terrible deed Nikanor killed both her and himself. Suddenly she saw this short-legged thief as he really was—and he became hateful to her. She could not love him—she had never really loved him. Now it was impossible to think of the man without feeling shame, aversion, despair. The prophecy of the terrible barefoot old man had come true. She felt herself infected, as it were, with some shameful incurable disease, and for ever separated from her father by a bottomless chasm.

As she went on musing, crying quietly, taking the kerchief off her head and smoothing it, her heart overflowed while her thoughts grew more and more vague. She remembered how she had loved, awaited someone —and how this love had been returned—and nowhere could she find refuge from anguish over the past, from pity for herself, from tenderness for him whom she had dreamed so long of loving. She thought of her father to whom she had once said, "I'm all on the outside," and she was ready to cry out, to run to his room, to fling herself at his feet, that he might stamp upon her, crush her under his boots, if only that would assuage her torment at the thought of the old days irretrievably lost. "For you, daughter, for you alone,"—she recalled his tender words and she wept, growing faint with passionate sorrow and tears.

One evening Ustin and Volodya left for the village together to have their hair cut. The evening was clear and peaceful; the flat expanse of ripe rye beyond the great road appeared rose-yellow in the luminous twilight; black arrowlike swallows, their tiny ruddy breasts glowing, flew past the open window at which Parashka sat. Suddenly, on the horizon, up from the rye field, rose the short figure of Nikanor; apparently he had been sitting in the rye hiding and had just risen and straightened himself up. He walked rapidly across the dry wheel-ruts and entered the house.

"Hello," he said in a low voice, pausing near the threshold. "No one at home?"

"No one," Parashka answered, her pale lips scarcely moving.

"We have some business to do. Let's go behind the house, under the oaks."

He spoke as a husband speaks, as an intimate endowed with some power, as a man with whom she already had an indissoluble and secret bond. She understood that it was not for business alone that he had called her. And suddenly, with a sweet agony, her heart sank again at the stark power of his command, at the presentiment that what had seemed so terrible to her the first time would happen again. And silently she rose and followed him.

Then all the while glancing around, he told her firmly, abruptly, why he had come. She must help him take two mares from her father's stable and run away with him to Rostov. She did not appear surprised and answered calmly, without lifting her eyes, "Very well."

The sun was sinking below the bearded ears of rye, where they sat by a hedge, and poured upon them a golden dust. From the great road, from the southeast, there blew the faint breeze of approaching July, the harvest time, when the deep dull blues of the sky are unchanging, and the droning insects with harsh wings descend on the rye and rock on its wind-blown ears.

Nikanor went on to say that within a week Ustin

would leave one night for the Tikhvinsk fair. He would take Volodya with him and would not return until late the next night. Nikanor was sure of this, for he had promised Ustin that he also would be at the fair to help him sell a stallion. This meant that during dinner time, when not a soul was likely to be about in the fields, it would be possible to take the mares, and hitching them to the cart, drive them quickly away in the direction of Lebedyani, keeping to the by-roads, which were generally untraveled until the busy harvest season arrived. At night they would find shelter in secret places—amid the grain, where the devil himself wouldn't think of looking for them. With daylight they would proceed farther. In Lebedyani he had a loyal crony with a heart of gold, who would dispose of the mares for him for three or four hundred rubles. They would then have over five hundred rubles, which would enable them to reach Rostov, where they would begin a business he had had long in mind.

"What sort of business?" Parashka asked.

"You are curious, aren't you?" said Nikanor with a smile.

"It had better be done by night," she said earnestly.

"What's come over you?" said Nikanor scornfully, rolling a cigarette with a piece of newspaper. He sighed. "No, my girl, that wouldn't work out. You'd better follow my plan."

"Isn't it possible to do it sooner?" Parashka asked, her eyes on her small bare feet.

"Act in haste, repent at leisure."

She made no reply, but in her heart hatred flamed up against him. To wait a whole week! Didn't he have enough feeling to understand her torments? Wouldn't it be better to hang herself at once on this oak?—she thought, but without putting her thought into so many words; and she began to bite her lips hard, to keep her face muscles from trembling. But she could not control herself and burst into tears.

"What's the matter with you?" Nikanor asked in astonishment.

She made no reply, and only wept the more bitterly.

"I spoke to you, didn't I?" he shouted gruffly.

"Let me alone!" She shouted back with such hatred and ferocity that Nikanor actually moved away from her.

"All right—enough, enough," he said, nonplussed. "But it would be much better if we discussed this business—"

And she stopped crying, and sat like one stupefied. . . .

For a whole week, until the time for the Tikhvinsk fair, Ustin, as if out of spite, stayed at home. Evgenya came—to complain of her soldier husband, who after his term of military service now turned out to be a complete fool and drunkard, and of her lame mother-in-law, who was evil and dissolute, and had her father-in-law completely under her thumb. But even Evgenya did not disconcert Parashka, who no longer thought, no longer felt. In her stupefaction, a sense of fateful sin overcame her, endued her with a shameless calm. She slept a great deal during the week, both day and night. Every time she awoke, she would jump up, dumfounded by the thought of what was almost immediately ahead of her.

At last the final night came.

It was singularly like the night when she had watched the campfire flaring beyond the great road. Now, as then, as she lay in the dark room, she saw through the window the nocturnal sky all studded with pale stars. And now, as then, her father was saying something in a passionate voice outside the window. Suddenly the door of the house was noiselessly pushed open.

"Daughter, are you asleep?" he asked in a low tone, as he paused near the threshold.

"No—" she murmured with difficulty.

Not noticing her strange tone, he moved toward the plank bed upon which she lay. He found her in the darkness, sat down near her, and laid a hand on her half-naked shoulder. His hand trembled.

"Daughter, what's the matter with you?" he asked quietly and solemnly, bending toward her face. She felt the touch of his beard, the warmth of his pleasant breath, and the pleasant rye odor of vodka. "Now don't hide anything from me," he said, embracing her, the coarse cloth of his peasant's coat scratching her shoulder. "You're young, warm-blooded—"

Her heart fluttered. "Father!" she wanted to cry out in a voice full of tears—and in the single cry to put all her anguish and helplessness. "Father—" she wanted to say—"he's ruined me, he's shamed me! I don't love him, I don't know whom I love! I wouldn't leave you for anyone in the world—" He drew still closer to her and suddenly whispered in quite a different tone, ingratiatingly, caressingly: "Would you like to have a little present? A new dress, maybe? I'm going to town now, to the fair—what would you like to have me buy you? Eh? Be quick now, don't be afraid—"

And his trembling hand passed down her back. Dumfounded, she struggled away from him, so that he almost fell from the bench on which he sat. She jumped to her feet and retreated to a corner, holding up her arms to ward him off. He stepped back, murmuring, "What's got into you? What is it? Why do you act like this?"

"Go away—" she spoke barely audibly, conscious that her lips were stiff. And, in a daze of joy, in a paroxysm of rapture, despair, she thought, "A-ah! So that's how it is!"

He stood there for a few moments, then went out. She heard his voice unnaturally loud out of doors, heard the creaking of the cart, and the neighing of the shying stallion tied to the cart, and then she heard her father and Volodya climb into the cart and set off. With feline keenness of sight she peered into the darkness of the house, that had become, as it were, transparent, and at the pale stars in the heavenly dome visible through the open window. For a long time she stood upon the plank bed, in the dead silence of night in the steppe that surrounded her. Then she lay down cautiously and at once fell asleep.

She awoke to a heavy, scorching, dazzling day; in the sultriness the shining horizon looked hazy and whitish. When she opened her eyes, it was already almost lunch time. The sun beat down upon the dim fly-specked windows, filled the house with heat and light. Scarcely awake, without stopping to wash, her head heavy with stupor, she ran barefooted to the threshold and stood in the sun. It was already high in the heavens, and the stark heat poured over her from head to foot. The sea of ripe grain, with its thick, dimly gleaming dust, seemed to have moved closer, erecting a solider barrier against the farmyard and the road. And in the dense hot air this dust color of the rye, its heavy ears bowed low and stiff in the silence, gave the impression of terrible, suffocating heat.

As in a daze, she glanced round her and tried hard to remember. What was she to do now? Last night, after her father's departure, it had seemed as if all of a sudden everything had become clear, simple, decided. Yet now, despite all her efforts, she could not remember just what it was that had been decided or in what way. That someone would shortly come to get her, and that it would be necessary to leave as soon as possible when this happened, and that she would have to hide, all this she recalled. But how had it happened that she had not bidden her father good-bye, had not said to him what she had thought of in the night, and what it was necessary to say? True, after what had happened yesterday, she might go without saying good-bye, without a word; but how came it that she had given no thought to what she ought to take with her? She had not gathered her things together, nor had she taken the trouble to wash or dress. Confused and stupefied, she remained standing in the sultry heat with uncovered head; she pressed her hands under her armpits and felt the heat on her naked shoulders, while her bare feet touched the hot stone of the threshold. The white dog was lying, with his tongue hanging out, in the short shadow of the storehouse. Frightened she glanced now at him, now at the rye, now at the by-road. . . .

Then suddenly, above the rye, against the dim, silvery horizon, appeared the shaft-bow of a cart, framing the head of a tall lean horse. Nikanor sat high at the front of his cart, his cap pushed back over the nape of his neck, and pulled at the taut reins. Urging his horse to a trot, and raising the dust, he turned sharply in, and the rattling cart rolled up to the very threshold. His eyes were dilated, his dark sunburned face was all in a sweat, his face had a strange expression—as if of astonishment.

"Well, you?" he said in a rapid whisper, as he jumped down from the cart, without noticing that Parashka was barefoot and almost naked. "Everything ready? Have they left?"

Without answering, she glared savagely at him, sprang away from the threshold and with flashing bare feet went toward the farmyard gates, in the direction of the stalls. Pressing her hot shoulder heavily against the gates, she pushed them open creaking before her. She walked across the deep dried manure, up to the dark stalls of the mares. Nikanor followed her, leading his horse to the gates and muttering, "But why haven't you put your clothes on?" On the door to stalls hung a large padlock. Parashka turned round.

"I haven't got a key," she said, staring at Nikanor with large, motionless, transparently green eyes.

Nikanor glanced round him and caught sight of the stone upon which the axes were sharpened. Snatching it up in both hands, he struck with it at the padlock.

The lock flew off together with the hinge—and Parashka caught it in the air and held it tight in her small sunburned hand. Nikanor pushed his cap still further back on the nape of his neck and, wet with sweat, with a bridle in one hand, he entered the stalls; lowering his head he peered into the darkness, where, pressing against the wall with lowered head, stood a bay mare, a beauty with lilac-colored eyes. Parashka took a long step and, awkwardly but with her whole strength, struck Nikanor across the temple with the lock. He stumbled sharply and fell, his head striking the manure. Parashka jumped away, and flew like an arrow out of the enclosure back through the gates. As she passed, Nikanor's horse took fright and dashed beside her into the road. The dust rose, the cart rattled, and the horse took the road toward town, toward the whitish shining distance beyond the crest of a hill. Parashka turned in another direction, across the road, through the rye. As she ran she glanced behind her and suddenly paused, for there was Nikanor, capless, his face and shirt red with blood, rushing out through the gates, Stumbling, he started off after the frightened horse. Parashka gave a piercing scream and then plunged into the dense suffocating rye. . . .

The peasants who drove their carts that day along the by-roads saw her running rapidly here and there in the pathless depths of the rye. Now she crouched down to rest, and peered out—and again she ran on, her head uncovered and her white chemise flashing in the sun.

It was five days before they caught her. As she tried to fight off her pursuers she seemed endowed with terrific strength, and savagely bit three peasants who twisted her arms in the effort to bind her with a new rein.